ILLEGAL CONTACT

BECKY HARMON

BELLA
B O O K S

2017

Bella Books, Inc.
P.O. Box 10543
Tallahassee, FL 32302

Printed in the United States of America on acid-free paper.

First Bella Books Edition 2017

Editor: Katherine V. Forrest
Cover Designer: Judith Fellows

ISBN: 978-1-59493-551-0

Other Bella Books by Becky Harmon

Tangled Mark
New Additions

Acknowledgments

Many thanks to Linda and Jessica Hill for continuing to publish the books I write. I'm very proud to be a part of Bella. I'm in excellent company.

Thank you to Judy and everyone who contributed to making this cover awesome.

Thank you, Katherine, for making my book tighter and more enjoyable for the readers.

Thanks to the production team at Bella for all the work you do behind the scenes.

To my co-workers for listening to me ramble about my stories, I owe you all. And Kathy, of course, for the creative title. Keep 'em comin'.

Thank you, Angela, for being my eager first reader and for wrapping my ankles before every game. Your encouragement keeps me going. To Coach Noodle—thank you for introducing me to the world of women's tackle football. Any team is lucky to have your enthusiasm and expertise. I love you but I will never do another bear crawl for as long as I live. To the women who give their hearts and soul to play football in the Women's Football Alliance. Your dedication is appreciated.

And most important, thank you readers, for taking a chance on each book I write. I truly hope you enjoy this one. I certainly enjoyed writing it. Please check out and support your local women's tackle football team. Between the Women's Football Alliance, WFA, and the Independent Women's Football League, IWFL, there are almost one hundred teams nationally.

About the Author

Becky Harmon was born and raised just south of the Mason-Dixon Line. Though she considers herself to be a Northerner, she moved south in search of warmth. Romance has always been her first love and when she's not writing it, she's reading it. Both of her previous published works, *Tangled Mark* and *New Additions*, are available from Bella Books. You can reach Becky at beckyharmon2015@yahoo.com.

Dedication

For Demi
To all the girls who dream of playing on a larger stage.
Anything is possible.

CHAPTER ONE

Jamison Krews rolled over and grabbed her buzzing cell phone from the nightstand.

"Krews," she mumbled into the phone.

"James," a familiar voice spoke urgently in her ear. "I need your help."

Jamison sat up pushing the comforter away from her body. Her head was fuzzy from sleep but the urgency in the voice quickly cleared the cobwebs.

"Mel? What's wrong?"

Mel Carter was one of the few people in her life she would call a friend. She had often told her and she had meant it, whatever...whenever...she needed anything, she would be there for her. Apprehension flooded her as she realized Mel was about to call in that promise.

"It's my sister. I think she's in danger. I need you to take care of her until I can get there."

"Okay. Fill me in." Jamison punched the speaker button and laid the phone on her dresser. Grabbing black pants and a button-down shirt from the closet she pulled them on over the boxers and tank top she'd slept in.

"The Tigers received threats naming Shea personally and Mom is freaking out. Shea isn't taking the threats seriously so she contacted Vince. He promised to send someone to stay with her. I wish it could be me but I'm in Afghanistan and I can't walk away from this mission yet." She sighed. "Maybe by the end of the week."

Jamison wet her hands and ran them through her shoulder-length hair pushing it back out of her eyes. Vince Flagler, founder of Flagler Security and Mel and Jamison's boss, was a master at threat analysis. If he agreed, then there was something to be concerned about. She had met Shea Carter one time about eight years ago. She had just led her high school football team through the playoffs and they were headed for the state finals. At eighteen, she was cocky and arrogant, with the same intensely dark eyes that seemed to run in Mel's family.

Mel's eyes had captured Jamison on her first day of work at Flagler Security. As her training officer, Mel had taken to Jamison and taught her everything she could. Which meant a lot, she had later learned. Mel hated being a training officer and preferred to work alone. She had refused every training assignment until Jamison. She was honored that Mel would turn to her to protect her sister but she also knew protecting someone who didn't want to be protected wouldn't be easy.

"What about Nikki?" Jamison had run into Mel and her latest fling, Nikki Mitchell, last month at the Flagler office in Pensacola and she wondered if Mel had already dumped her.

"She's with me." Mel sighed again. "Please, James. I know what I'm asking. Shea will be difficult. She's headstrong and can be a real ass sometimes." She paused. "But she's my baby sister and I love her. I need someone who can stand up to her and keep her safe despite her protests."

"You know I'll do it, Mel. Are the Tigers back in Tallahassee yet? I know they played Boston yesterday."

"You mean stomped Boston. Yes, they got in last night."

"I'll head over there now. I'll call you when I get a handle on what's going on."

"Thank you so much." Jamison could hear the relief in Mel's voice. "If I don't answer leave a message and I'll call you as soon as I can."

* * *

Jamison pulled her Ford Explorer into the parking lot outside the Tallahassee Tigers football stadium. Tallahassee University had opened in the late eighteen hundreds with fifty students and today it enrolled approximately forty thousand. The main campus stretched over a thousand acres with additional buildings placed throughout town. Last year, it had been listed in the top fifty public universities nationwide.

She maneuvered the small pickup into a spot by gate B, staring up at the marquee that announced the Tigers latest win. They were undefeated. One more regular season game and they would head to the conference championship. Jamison followed the Tigers as avidly as anyone who lived in this town. It was hard not to since pretty much everyone was a diehard fan especially now that they were winning. The Tigers hadn't won a championship in almost thirty years and they had never had an undefeated season. Or a female quarterback.

Jamison remembered Mel telling her how hard it had been for Shea once she graduated from high school. She was the star quarterback and had she been male she probably would have been drafted straight into the National Football League. As a female, no one wanted her. There had been one or two offers from small colleges willing to sign her if she switched to special teams but Shea wouldn't buckle under the pressure.

Her path to the Tigers had been widely publicized by all the sports media outlets. She maintained her skills by practicing and helping to coach a women's semi-pro tackle football team. After several years, she enrolled in a community college that agreed to let her practice with the team. At the end of her first year, they put her on the roster and allowed her to dress for games, but still wouldn't let her play. When their starting quarterback was injured, Shea stepped in to lead them to multiple wins. They begged her to stay but Shea chose to attempt a walk-on with the

Tigers. They too had resisted but her diligence had finally paid off in her senior year and the Tigers were reaping the benefits.

Jamison ran a hand through her hair as she slid from the truck and headed for the administration offices. Her boots echoed on the cement floors as she maneuvered the maze of hallways behind the stadium. Approaching Coach Sutton's door, she could hear raised voices. She lifted her hand to knock but froze when a female voice caught her attention.

"I don't care what my sister said. I do not want or need a babysitter!"

"Shea, be reasonable. It's for your own safety," a male voice countered.

"Reasonable! I'll give you reasonable."

"Stop it now, Carter," another male voice interrupted Shea's rant. "This conversation is over. A protection detail is being sent by Flagler and you *will* cooperate with them or you won't play this weekend. Understood?"

"Understood."

Jamison thought the last word had definitely been forced out between gritted teeth but she didn't have time to think about it as the door was flung open and she was pushed backward from the impact. She placed her hands on Shea's waist and pushed her away as she widened her stance to keep from falling into the wall. Dark eyes raked over her body before coming to rest on her face. A seductive smile spread across Shea's face. Then she turned and walked away. Jamison watched her lengthen her stride with each step as she rounded the corner out of sight.

She took a deep breath, tapped lightly on the doorframe and stepped into the office. "Jamison Krews. I was sent by Flagler Security."

The man behind the desk nodded. "Ronald Sutton." Jamison recognized the coach of the Tallahassee Tigers from many televised football games.

She turned to the other man who wore a campus security uniform. "Carlton Hammer." His grip was strong but he released quickly and she smiled as she realized who he was.

"The Hammer?"

His smile widened as she referenced his nickname when he was the star running back for the Tallahassee Tigers.

"I don't hear that much anymore."

She nodded. "Well, it certainly fits." He wasn't much taller than her five foot eight but his muscular width made up for his lack of height. His biceps and thighs bulged through the polyester uniform and he seemed to have lost no muscle in the twenty years since he played ball.

Sutton motioned to one of the chairs in front of his desk. "Have a seat." He looked at Carlton. "Can you make her a copy of the file?"

"Sure. I'll be right back." Carlton departed quickly.

Sutton removed the Tigers ball cap and rubbed his bald head. "She's not happy with this arrangement."

"So I heard."

"Yeah, Carlton thought if he broke it to her gently she might take it better." He chuckled. "Not likely."

She couldn't help but smile. "Her cooperation would be nice but it's not necessary."

He nodded. "I guess you want to hear the details, right?" He continued, "It began after our second game. There was a note waiting in the locker room. The police have the original but Carlton kept a copy. The letters were cut out of magazines and pasted into a creepy message. Basically it said stop winning or else. We filed a police report but no one really took it seriously. I mean, come on." He shrugged and rubbed his face. "After each win there was a new note. The police tried to stake out the stadium and when that didn't work they tried blocking the entrances to keep anyone from coming inside. We couldn't use cameras because, well, it was a locker room. Somehow the notes continued to arrive. Like I said no one was really taking it serious."

"But something changed?"

"Yeah, after our sixth win there wasn't a note. Or at least none we could find. We thought he'd given up. Our seventh game was at home but it was being nationally televised so we put the team up in a hotel the night before. The brakes went out on the bus driving them back to the stadium the next day. Luckily the driver was able to wedge the bus in a narrow alley before it crashed into something or someone. We won that game and the next day the note was back and even more disturbing. The investigation found the brakes had been tampered with. That's when the police started taking the threats more seriously."

"When did it become focused on Ms. Carter?"

"After the last game," Carlton said, returning with a thick manila folder, which he passed to Jamison. "She uses the women's shower room down the hall before and after games. Normally, I have an officer patrolling the hallway so she doesn't get harassed by the media but we had a fight in the student section. I had to pull everyone to get it cleared up before the cameras caught it." Carlton shook his head in disgust. "They'll film anything and it just makes the school look bad."

Sutton took over again. "I didn't notice she wasn't in the locker room for the pre-game meeting but when we took the field no one could find her. I sent one of the coaches to look for her but the door was locked and she didn't answer his knocks."

"Coach called me and I unlocked the door," Carlton said. "Poor thing was locked inside the equipment closet in the back of the locker room. Screaming like crazy."

Sutton laughed. "Yeah, that poor thing went on a rampage against Georgia Tech. I've never seen her so pissed."

Jamison smiled remembering the fiery look in Shea's eyes when they had collided earlier. She watched the smile quickly fade from Sutton's face, his features turning hard as he spoke.

"This morning's note rambled about women being kept in their proper places and Shea would be the first to go. Last Saturday was only a sample to show us how easy it'll be to take her out."

Jamison understood his frustration, and she was itching to read the file for herself. It sounded like Shea was in real danger. "Is there anyone watching her right now?"

"Yes, the Tallahassee PD has an officer tailing her from a distance. She's been told to stay in her townhouse when she is not in class or at practice. Though I doubt she's listening."

Jamison nodded. "I need to run a few errands and then I'll relieve the officer." She tapped the folder and looked at Carlton. "Once I review this, I'll let you know if I need additional information."

He nodded. "Anything I can do to help. I wrote my cell number on the inside cover or call me at the office."

She stood and shook Sutton's hand. "Focus on football, Coach." She winked at Carlton. "We got this."

CHAPTER TWO

Jamison showered and dressed in blue jeans and a silk jersey T-shirt, pulling on her dark blue blazer to cover her shoulder holster. She packed enough clothes to get her through the week. Then she drove through the hanging moss-covered streets to Shea's townhouse. Three blocks from the main campus, Shea's street was a mix of residential and small offices. She parked behind the TPD patrol car and walked around to his window. She showed him her identification and told him he was cleared to go. He was eager to return to regular duty and assured Jamison that Shea was inside the townhouse.

She walked around the house getting familiar with her surroundings. There was a backdoor but it went into the privacy-fenced backyard and the only gate outside the fence was adjacent to the front door. It seemed unlikely Shea would climb the privacy fence but Jamison wasn't going to assume she wouldn't.

She returned to her truck and stared at the two-story white duplex. She made a mental note to find out who lived in the other half of the building. The window curtain on the second floor opened and Jamison could see a figure inside watching her. She pulled the manila folder from the truck and crossed to the red-trimmed door. Before she could knock the door was flung open and she stared into the fiery dark eyes of Shea Carter.

"Nice to see you again," Shea said sarcastically. "I guess you're my babysitter."

Jamison slid past her into the townhouse, tossed her folder on the dining room table and turned to face Shea. "I'm Jamison Krews and I'm here at your sister's request."

Shea frowned. "Didn't we meet a couple years ago?"

Jamison nodded. "You'd just won the playoffs."

"Oh yes. I remember. My sister's fling of the moment."

Jamison rolled her eyes. "I'm not here to talk about your sister's love life. I'm here because your sister asked me to come and because your life has been threatened."

"It was a prank. Probably a rival team trying to mess with us," Shea said, flopping onto the couch and switching on the television. "Everyone is just overreacting."

Jamison leaned against the table and studied her profile. Shea's short dark hair was curly and cut above her ears. Jamison couldn't stop her gaze from drifting up the long legs to where the bottom of the blue gym shorts hugged her thighs. Then she caught herself. This was not going the way she had planned it. Time for her to take control of the situation. She grabbed the remote from where it lay on Shea's stomach and switched off the television. Crossing her arms over her chest she faced Shea.

"Here's how things are going to work. You're not going to leave this house without telling me where you're going. I'll be with you twenty-four hours a day. I'll do my best to stay out of your business. Your sister hopes to be here by the end of the week and then I'll disappear." She tossed the remote back onto Shea's stomach and took a seat at the dining room table. Opening the file, she began reading the police reports.

After a few minutes, the ominously silent Shea got up and disappeared up the stairs. Jamison truly hoped she didn't try to climb out a window but she listened closely just in case.

* * *

What a load of shit! Shea pulled her running shoes from her closet and slammed the door shut. Punching Mel's number on her cell phone she waited for voice mail to pick up and left a scathing message with as many curse words as she could think to include. She would make her sister pay for this. Dialing her mother with one hand, she pulled on her running shoes.

"Mom, I'm going to kill Mel. This is such bullshit."

"Shea Elizabeth, you will not talk to me like that. I don't care how upset you are."

"Sorry, Mom." Shea stopped pacing and dropped onto the bed. "I can't believe Mel called the cavalry. How can I focus on football when I have someone invading my space? You know I need to be alone when I'm preparing. This weekend's game is really important. I can't afford to be distracted."

"Are you finished, Shea?"

"Yeah, I guess I am."

"I'm the one that called Mr. Flagler so don't blame your sister. We're all worried and want you to be safe. Just focus on football and let Flagler deal with your safety. I'm sure whoever they sent will be professional and not invade your space."

"She's already invading my space. And she's ordering me around like I'm a child."

"Well, you should do what she says, honey. I'm coming down for the game this weekend so we can talk about it then if you're still unhappy."

"Fine. But I'm going to the gym to work out now and she better not have a problem with it."

Shea heard her mother sigh and she grimaced. Even to herself she sounded like a four-year-old throwing a tantrum.

"Please be cooperative, Shea. I'll talk to you soon. I love you, baby."

"Love you too, Mom."

Shea slid the phone into the pocket of her shorts. She ignored Jamison as she passed and had her hand on the front door before Jamison spoke.

"Where are you going?"

"The gym."

Jamison stood, pulling keys from her pocket. "Fine. We'll take my truck."

She didn't respond or wait to see if Jamison would follow. "Figures you drive a truck," she mumbled under her breath.

* * *

Jamison unlocked the doors and climbed behind the wheel. She watched Shea out of the corner of her eye as she drove. Shea gave one word directions making it clear she didn't intend to have a conversation but Jamison attempted to engage her anyway.

"Aren't you too sore from the game to work out today?"

Shea shook her head.

"Is this a scheduled team event?"

Shea shook her head again.

"I'll accompany you inside but I'll try to avoid drawing attention."

Shea shrugged as she turned to look at her. "That'll be hard with you dressed like that."

Jamison frowned. "What's wrong with how I'm dressed?"

"You look like a professor."

She cringed at Shea's words. Too late to change now.

"Can you at least take off the blazer?" Shea asked.

"Unfortunately, no." She wouldn't even consider not carrying her pistol and there was no need to discuss it with Shea.

"Fine. Don't talk to me then." Shea pointed to a set of double doors. "Let me off there."

"No." Jamison backed into a nearby parking space. "I'll agree to keep my distance but only if you don't try to lose me."

"Whatever." Shea jumped from the truck as soon as it stopped moving.

Jamison cut the engine and followed her. She watched Shea's calf muscles flex as she trotted up the stairs. Shea had to be over six feet tall and she didn't slouch at all like tall women often did.

She walked with her shoulders back and Jamison admired her confidence.

Shea pulled open a metal-framed glass door and Jamison could hear the clanking of weight machines. She paused for a moment giving Shea time to make her appearance before she pulled open the door and followed her inside. The room was large and split into three sections. The first section held only cardio machines, treadmills, bicycles, steppers and a few rowing machines. The second section was filled with free weights and weight lifting machines. The third section was empty but the floor was covered with mats for stretching and floor exercises. Ten or so college-aged men worked out on the free weights and Jamison glanced at each one. They all seemed intent on their workouts and not at all focused on each other or on Shea. Jamison saw Coach Sutton and another man, tall and lanky, inside the glass office in the rear of the room and she headed toward them after locating Shea on a treadmill.

"Hey Coach," Jamison said, sticking her head in the door of the office.

"How's things going?" He stood, shook her hand and then introduced her to the other man. "Ben is one of my assistant coaches. Jamison is Carter's new bodyguard."

Ben smiled and shook her hand. "Not a soul jealous of that job."

Jamison smiled as she moved to where she could watch Shea and continue the conversation. "We're getting along fine so far. I've agreed to keep my distance and she's agreed to not try to sneak away from me." Jamison rolled her eyes. "I think."

Both men laughed. Sutton handed her a security access badge. "Carlton and I were thinking you might need that to get around." He smiled. "In case she *accidentally* loses you."

Jamison nodded. "Thanks. I'm sure it will come in handy." She stepped toward the door. "I'll see you gentlemen later."

"Feel free to use the workout equipment whenever you're in here," Sutton called to her. "Also, practice is every afternoon from two to six." He smiled again. "In case she doesn't tell you."

She grinned. "Thanks for the information."

She located an unused bench in the corner of the room and crossed to it. Turning the red plastic bench so she could see the entire room, she straddled it and pulled her phone from her pocket. She logged into her email and checked her new messages. After returning a few emails, she opened an Internet browser and typed in Shea Carter's name.

Out of the corner of her eye, she saw Shea move from the treadmill to a rowing machine. She had pulled off her T-shirt and wore only a black sports bra with her gym shorts. Jamison's eyes were drawn to Shea's chest as her arms worked back and forth. Her breasts were small and firm against the muscles in her chest. Jamison could see the outline of her nipples clearly through the thin material as it stretched across her chest with each stroke.

Wishing she had brought a bottle of water, Jamison licked her dry lips, pulling her gaze up Shea's body to her face. She was taken aback to see the dark eyes staring back at her. Jamison tried to casually look away but knew she had been caught. If she wanted to gain Shea's trust, she would need to be more professional and avoid ogling her body. Even if she was beautiful. She did her best not to stare directly at Shea and instead browsed the Internet following every link Shea's name had brought up.

Finally, after several hours, Shea appeared to be winding down. She flopped onto one of the stretching mats with her back to Jamison. A slender blonde in khaki pants and a Tallahassee Tigers shirt joined her. Jamison watched the woman help Shea slowly work through multiple stretches covering every muscle in her body. Their voices were soft as they chatted and Jamison pushed aside a ridiculous twinge of jealousy at their familiarity. When they finished, Shea headed for the exit. Jamison stood and followed her. The other woman smiled as she passed but didn't offer a greeting.

* * *

Shea was exhausted but she still had several hours of studying to do before she crashed for the night. As she stood by Jamison's truck watching her cross the parking lot, she thought about the look of admiration she had caught on Jamison's face earlier. She was not ready to admit she found this woman intriguing. Attractive, yes, and maybe a little mysterious. She was also bossy and annoying but mostly she brought out the whiner in her and she despised that. She was not a child anymore and stomping her feet in a tantrum would not accomplish anything or gain her any respect. Her breath caught as the early evening sun reflected off something metallic inside Jamison's blazer. A gun. No wonder she wouldn't take off her blazer. Shea was struck by the implied seriousness of her situation. Maybe she should be more careful.

* * *

Closing the folder, Jamison sat back in her chair pushing her hands through her hair. At this point the police had no suspects and no leads on the threat to Shea. Her job wasn't to solve this case but the sooner she figured things out the sooner she could go home. The house was quiet and every move Jamison made seemed to echo throughout the room. Shea had sequestered herself upstairs since their return about three hours earlier. She had mumbled something about studying but when Jamison looked into her face she saw exhaustion and she doubted any work was being accomplished. Her stomach growled and she looked at her watch. It was almost six and she hadn't eaten all day.

She opened every cabinet in the small kitchen and stared at the lone jar of peanut butter. What in the world did this woman eat? She made a mental note to grab some groceries while Shea was in class tomorrow. Closing the cabinets, she began searching the drawers for take-out menus and quickly decided on Chinese over pizza. While she was deciding whether to interrupt Shea and see if she wanted anything, the doorbell rang. Immediately, footsteps sounded on the stairs. Jamison pulled her pistol and cautiously stepped toward the front door. Holding the pistol beside her leg, she attempted to catch a glimpse of their visitor through the blinds. She heard Shea approach behind her.

"What the hell are you doing? It's just the damn delivery boy." She pushed past Jamison and swung open the door.

Jamison quickly stepped between Shea and the deliveryman, taking in the pizza box in his arms and the pimples on his face. Clearing the kid as a threat, she quickly scanned the street in front of the house before holding a hand out behind her. "Money?"

Shea slapped some bills into Jamison's hand and leaned around her. "Hey Jimmy. Thanks for being so quick."

"No…no problem," Jimmy stuttered, his eyes on the pistol at Jamison's side. "Uh…uh…everything okay, Ms. Shea?"

"Yeah, it's fine," Shea said, pushing Jamison to the side and grabbing the pizza box from Jimmy's hands. "Keep the change," she called as she turned and headed for the stairs with the box.

Jamison gave the driver a dismissive nod and closed the door, holstering her weapon. She shook her head. Clearly she and Shea were on their way to becoming the best of friends. She pulled out her phone and dialed the number for the Chinese restaurant.

She paced in front of the door until her food arrived, opening it before the driver could ring the bell. She took her food to the table and ate while she jotted notes on a legal pad. She wanted to meet with the TPD officer in charge of the investigation. She added Officer Cannon to her notepad along with the station phone number. She wanted to know if the hotel had any surveillance cameras that might have caught someone tampering with the bus brakes.

She was finishing her dinner when she heard footsteps in the hallway above her. Shea was moving in the opposite direction of the stairs, either getting ready for bed or making an escape. When she heard her return to the bedroom and close the door, she retrieved the bag from the truck that she had packed. Exploring the downstairs, she discovered a bedroom next to the bathroom. The bed was made but there were no clothes in the dresser or closet. Jamison took that as a good sign that she wasn't stealing a roommate's bed or that she'd have an unwelcome visitor in the night.

CHAPTER THREE

Jamison lay wrapped in a quilted blanket she had found beside the couch. It was warm and it smelled like lavender. She squeezed her eyes shut hoping to block out the visions of Shea that were playing through her mind. She could almost feel Shea's lean muscular body beneath her fingers. She pulled her fingers into a fist and then released them, rubbing her face. Fantasizing about Shea in her black sports bra would not help her focus on her job.

Instead she remembered Shea's hostile attitude the previous night. Jamison knew she needed to take a more professional approach. Shea's beauty was certainly irrelevant to her assignment. She could hear Mel's voice in her head chastising her for her behavior and she smiled. Good thing Mel didn't know where her thoughts had been. She was thinking about a shower when she heard footsteps on the stairs. She waited as they entered the kitchen and then she heard the front door slam.

"No fucking way!" Jamison jumped to her feet and slid into her running shoes, thankful for the shorts and T-shirt she had decided to sleep in. She quickly pulled a Windbreaker from the back of the door and pushed her pistol in the pocket. Charging out the front door, she caught sight of Shea turning the corner with her blue backpack slung over one shoulder. Jamison cursed under her breath as she hurried to make the corner before Shea could disappear.

* * *

Shea glanced over her shoulder as she rounded the corner toward campus. Jamison came running behind her, wearing shorts and running shoes. Her hair was disheveled and Shea tried not to think about how cute she looked. She would definitely blend in with the college students this morning. Shea had thought about knocking on Jamison's door when she came down the stairs but she was only going to class. She had planned to check in with Jamison before her noon class, but now she wouldn't need to do that. She would have time to grab lunch at the sub shop instead.

Shea waved to two classmates standing outside the door of her classroom and detoured past them. Ducking into the alcove in the stairway, she fed quarters into the coffee machine. It wasn't gourmet but better than nothing. Her last roommate had a coffeemaker and it was nice to have that each morning but she'd moved out over a month ago and taken her appliances with her. Shea had considered buying one for herself but knew she would drink more if she had it. Caffeine wasn't the best beverage for her and guilt pushed her to feed dollars into the next machine, punching the button for a bottled water. She dropped the water into her pack and took a sip of the coffee.

Her friends had already taken seats inside the classroom and she slid into a chair beside them as the professor walked into the room. Outside the door, she saw Jamison stroll by giving her a hard stare and she smiled until she saw the annoyed look on her face. She hadn't meant to make Jamison angry and unfortunately there was nothing she could do about it now. She would think about apologizing later. It was against her nature to give in too easily.

She wondered if Jamison would be waiting when her class was over. She had to admit that she hoped so. Jamison was attractive and under different circumstances she would have actively pursued her. Jamison's short brown hair had a shaggy appearance and she liked the way Jamison ran her fingers through it when she pushed it out of her face. She had looked comfortable jogging to catch her this morning and she imagined her legs would be lean and toned. Mel took care of her body and exercised regularly so she had to believe most Flagler agents were the same. She looked forward to testing Jamison's endurance on a run tomorrow. She turned her attention to the professor.

* * *

Jamison waited until she was convinced Shea was settled into the classroom and then walked back to the duplex. She didn't understand why Shea insisted on being so difficult but the bottom line was she needed to get with it and stop being a step behind. She reached in her pocket to grab her cell phone and realized she had forgotten to grab it before leaving the house. She wanted to blame Shea but she knew it was her own fault. Her focus had been off since she arrived yesterday. She didn't want to admit it but Shea rattled her. Jamison knew beneath the spoiled kid exterior was a fascinating woman but not one she was allowed to be interested in. Even though Shea was barely four years younger than her, she was here to do a job.

She started to jog but her bare feet rubbed the inside of her running shoes. She considered herself a runner but she had never been able to go without socks. Anxious to return to the duplex and get her plan together she ignored the blisters starting to form on the back of her heels. She took the four stairs leading up to the duplex in one leap but slammed to a stop when she turned the doorknob. It was locked and she didn't have a key. She took a deep breath and then checked all of the normal key hiding places on the porch. Walking around the house, she found the only window open was on the second floor.

The old-fashioned latticework lining the back of the house went right past the open window. Jamison shook her head and looked around to see which of the neighbors had a view of this location. She didn't want to have to explain her actions to the police. She walked around the house again and shook the thin white wood. Unfortunately, this seemed to be her best option so she began to climb. When she reached the window, she wrapped an arm through the lattice so she could use both hands to remove the screen. It was a standard screen easy to remove from the inside but not so easy from the outside. Missing the knife she usually carried, she pushed the screen to one side and stuck her fingernails inside the edge. She growled as her fingernails were pulled backward but she became more determined with each tug. Finally the screen popped loose and fell to the ground. She swung one leg over the windowsill and pulled herself inside.

She was standing in Shea's bedroom. She turned all the way around taking in the room. Shea's comforter was a light blue and green with a matching lamp and plush study chair in the corner. There was one picture on her dresser of Shea, Mel and their mother, standing on a beach with sparkling blue water behind them. Jamison stared into Shea's dark eyes and then turned away with a sigh. Another time. Another place. And someone else's sister, and she might be in luck.

She ran downstairs and retrieved the broken screen. Putting it back in place, she closed and locked Shea's window. She would have to replace it today but for now it would give the façade of being secure. She quickly showered and pulled on clean shorts and a T-shirt. Shea's Windbreaker had been comfortable and it would help her blend in so she pulled it on over her shoulder holster. Digging through the kitchen drawers, she found a ring of keys and tried them all until she found one that fit the front door.

She shoved the key in her pocket and jogged back to the classroom where she had left Shea. Students were pouring from the open door as she arrived so she leaned against the wall several doors down, hoping she looked more casual than she felt after her morning adventure. Shea spotted her as soon as she came into the hallway, gave her a smile and then walked in the opposite direction. Jamison followed her. Two buildings down and up a flight of stairs, Shea entered another identical classroom. Jamison waited until the professor began to talk and then she hurried to the security office. Carlton sat at his desk with a stack of paperwork in front of him.

"Hey, how's things going?" he greeted her.

She raised her eyebrows, not really wanting to relay her morning to anyone. "I've had better days." She smiled. "Can you get me a copy of Shea's class schedule?"

He chuckled. "Ducking out on you already?"

"No one said she'd be cooperative."

"That's for sure." He picked up the phone and dialed. "Eleanor, can you email me a copy of Shea Carter's class schedule?"

Jamison looked at the pictures on his wall as he talked sweetly to the woman in the registrar's office. There were several football pictures of The Hammer in action and a large aerial view of the Tallahassee Tigers football stadium.

Carlton's printer roared to life and he handed a single piece of paper to Jamison. "Here you go."

"Thanks. I really appreciate this." She turned to go and then spun back to him. "Is there anywhere near campus that sells hardware supplies? Shea needs a new screen in her bedroom window."

Carlton raised his eyebrows and picked up his phone, punching in a number. "I can take care of that too. It's a rental," he said as he waited for someone to pick up on the other end. "Hey Johnny, I need a window screen replaced in the duplex on Macomb Street."

"Upstairs bedroom," she added.

"Yeah, yeah, the upstairs bedroom." He paused and listened. "Great. Thanks, man."

"I really owe you now," she said. "I need to run before Ms. Carter gets out of class, but I really appreciate your help."

"No problem at all. I'll see you this afternoon at practice, right?"

"Yep, I'll see you there."

* * *

Shea glanced across the faces waiting in the hall outside her class. There was no sign of Jamison and she felt a little disappointed.

"Shea?" Mindi bumped her as they walked.

"What?" Shea growled. She hated to be pushed and Mindi knew it.

Mindi laughed. "I was asking if you wanted to hit the sub shop and you weren't answering."

"Yeah, sure. That's fine." She searched the faces on the stairs as they exited the building. Maybe Jamison was waiting out here. Her gaze locked on Jamison still wearing her Windbreaker and leaning against a building pillar. Jamison was talking on the phone but their eyes met and she gave Shea a nod.

"Why are you smiling?" Mindi frowned. "What's with you today?"

Mindi wasn't much more than a superficial friend and though she might suspect Shea was a lesbian it wasn't a conversation Shea would ever have with her. Telling her she was being tailed by a security agent was not on Shea's agenda either. Or that she thought the security agent was hot. She smiled at Mindi. "Well, I don't know…maybe I'm distracted by the biggest game of my life coming up."

"Oh right," Mindi said apologetically.

Shea felt a little guilty about making Mindi feel bad but it was partially true. She was more than a little anxious about the game this weekend but currently her focus was on the woman following her across campus.

* * *

Jamison left a voice mail message for TPD Officer Cannon asking her to meet with her tomorrow while Shea was in class. Then she dialed the Flagler office in Pensacola while she followed Shea away from campus.

"Hodges."

"Hey Todd. You're just the man I needed."

"Wow. I bet you don't get to say that often."

"Nice, buddy. That's really nice."

Todd laughed. "What do you need, Krews?"

"I need a couple outdoor surveillance cameras installed. Today preferably."

"Everyone always wants things now," he grumbled. "What city are you in?"

"Tallahassee."

"Okay. I'll let you know when they're installed and send you the password to access the video."

She gave him the address as she watched Shea enter a sub shop on Gaines Street a few blocks from campus. She leaned against the wall outside the entrance with a clear view of Shea inside. Glancing at her watch, she dialed Mel's cell phone.

"Give me some good news, James," Mel said, not bothering with a greeting.

"Good news…well let's see. She almost got the pizza boy shot last night, she snuck out this morning and I had to tail her in my pajamas." She paused dramatically. "And then she locked me out of the house and I had to climb in her bedroom window."

Mel laughed. "Shit, James. You must be loving my little sister."

Jamison laughed with her. "It's going fine so far. She's not happy so we're still working through a few things but she's safe." Jamison made eye contact with Shea through the restaurant window and their gazes held. "Seriously though, I've reviewed the file and hope to meet with the TPD officer tomorrow. Flagler is setting up some surveillance cameras around the house today."

"Thanks for the update. You have no idea how much it means to me that you're there protecting her. It looks like Nikki and I'll be back in the States for the game on Saturday but I don't have our schedule yet."

"Nikki, huh? Still holding on to that one?"

Mel was silent for a second and Jamison thought they had lost connection. Her voice was soft when she finally spoke. "Oh yeah, I'm gonna be holding on to this one for a while."

"That sounds serious. I look forward to grabbing a beer with you and getting all the details."

"Sounds like a plan. Oh and I talked with Mrs. Bowden. Vince had already briefed her so she's on board with your assignment. Call her if you need anything."

"Thanks. Hopefully I won't need to."

"Yeah, I hope that too. Take care, James. Of you and my little sister."

"I will." Jamison hit disconnect with her thumb.

CHAPTER FOUR

Jamison's stomach growled as the smells from inside the small shop wafted through the open door. She kept her focus on her phone as Shea and her friend walked past, and then fell into step behind them. They parted when they reached the edge of campus and Shea turned north toward Tennessee Street. Jamison lengthened her stride to match Shea but said nothing as they walked side by side. Several times she noticed Shea glance at her as if she wanted to say something and Jamison waited, remaining silent.

Finally as they approached the red brick building dominating the corner and stretching several floors above them, Shea stopped and turned toward her. "I was going to come back to the house at eleven after class."

Jamison said nothing and Shea began walking again.

"I wasn't trying to ditch you," she continued, an edge of anger in her voice. "Are you just not talking or are you really that mad at me."

"I'm not mad."

"Right."

Jamison looked at Shea and grinned. "Anymore."

Shea smiled back at her and Jamison enjoyed the glow it seemed to cast on her. She liked it when Shea smiled.

"Well, I just wanted to apologize. I'm not used to checking in with someone."

"I understand but I can't really keep you safe if I'm not with you."

Shea nodded and they walked the rest of the way in companionable silence. When they reached the building for Shea's class she said, "I'll go straight to the locker room after this class. Practice is at two."

"I'll wait for you here."

Shea nodded and entered the red brick building.

Jamison watched her disappear through the doors before turning toward the duplex. She had located an organic market on her phone earlier but needed her truck for the drive. She jogged lightly, trying to ignore the blisters that had formed on her feet. At the market, she grabbed ingredients for a few meals and then loaded the cart with fruits and vegetables.

Back at the duplex, she quickly stored the food and returned to the campus. Again she was reminded that she needed to bandage her blisters tonight.

She arrived on the steps as Shea emerged from the building. Shea was quiet as they walked toward the stadium and Jamison didn't disrupt her concentration. For the moment, at least, they seemed cohesive and she relaxed as Shea shortened her steps to match hers. It almost felt like they were walking together. Jamison had always been considered tall for a female but Shea had more than a couple of inches on her. Each time Shea punched a crosswalk button, Jamison studied her hand. She couldn't believe she hadn't noticed before how large her hands were and the length of her fingers. An asset for football. Jamison had a sudden urge to thread her fingers with Shea's and feel the strength in her hand. She pushed aside her rambling thoughts and concentrated on watching the people around her.

There were no security measures during the week to keep people out of the stadium. She made a mental note to talk with

Carlton about the positioning of the cameras in and around the stadium. In the locker room, she sat on a bench in the corner and tried to stay out of the way. She watched Shea switch to a moisture resistant T-shirt and her eyes roamed the muscles in her back until she pulled her shoulder pads, already covered in her practice jersey, over her head.

She didn't know much about preparation for a football practice or game but apparently today was a light day as Shea didn't exchange her shorts for football pants and pads. She tied the laces on her cleats and moved toward the door. Jamison followed her. Shea turned, stopping inches from Jamison.

Shea put her hand on the center of Jamison's chest. An electrical shock charged through her system.

"I am headed to the men's locker room and you might not want to follow me." Shea gave her a wink. "It can get really smelly in there."

Her chest burned where Shea's hand rested. She stared into Shea's face, enjoying the relaxed attitude and hint of flirting. She hadn't seen this side of Shea before and if they weren't about to join the entire Tallahassee Tigers football team she would bask in it. Instead she rolled her eyes, grasping Shea's hand and dropping it from her chest. "I'll take my chances." She nodded to the door. "Lead the way."

"I always do."

She shook her head and followed Shea through the men's locker room door, hanging back while Shea announced their presence. Shea took a seat facing the whiteboard and away from the men's lockers where they were still dressing. Jamison remained near the door, shielded from the locker room by the coach's office. She watched the guys joke with Shea as the chairs in front of the whiteboard slowly filled.

At exactly two p.m., Coach Sutton stepped out of his office, directing a nod at Jamison as he walked to the front of the locker room. Dead silence filled the room as everyone waited for him to speak. He briefly praised the team for their win on Saturday and moved immediately on to the upcoming game. Time moved slowly as he drew play after play on the board, moving the x's and o's from one spot to another. After about an hour, another coach stepped forward, gave a short prayer and then sent the team to the field. Jamison waited until everyone had exited and then slowly made her way down the tunnel and onto the field. She had never attended a Tigers game but she felt the years of tradition surrounding her.

She walked slowly into the sunlight-filled stadium and she could almost hear the roar of the crowd. She turned completely around looking at row after row of seating. How would she ever protect Shea during a game? She looked out across the field and saw Carlton Hammer sitting in the stands alone. She climbed the stairs and crossed to midfield, taking a seat beside him.

She searched the field and located Shea before leaning back in her chair.

Carlton's focus was on the field as he watched the players run through drills. "They do the same thing every time they come onto the field. Same drills. Same stretches. On game days they come onto the field and they do these same exercises. It's just another day for them. Coach Sutton has really molded them into a fine team."

She watched Shea pull out of a three-point stance and sprint twenty yards, her long legs carrying her past the teammates on either side of her. "Every game I've seen they appear so relaxed," she said. "Even now you can't tell by their behavior that they're about to break a thirty-year losing streak. There's none of the cockiness you normally see with winning teams."

"That's Coach Sutton. He doesn't tolerate the crap. They're each here to do a job and that's what he expects from them." He leaned back in his seat and stretched out his legs. He looked at her with a devilish grin. "Except for your kitten." His grin grew bigger and his teeth were almost fluorescent in the sunlight against his dark skin. "Coach babies her like she's royalty."

Jamison laughed. "Kitten?"

"We need a code word for her don't we? You know like the President is the eagle."

"I know what you mean, Carlton, but you do know what she'd do if she heard us calling her kitten?"

"How about cub then? Like a tiger cub."

Jamison laughed again. "Are you trying to piss her off?"

Carlton laughed too. "I've seen her pretty angry a time or two. She can shoot fire out of those dark eyes."

They both watched Shea take the snap from center, pivot and release a long spiral downfield to her receiver.

Carlton shook his head. "But she sure can throw that ball. I was here the day she arrived as a walk-on."

Jamison glanced at him. This was a story she wanted to hear. "You were?"

He nodded. "She was real quiet. Didn't talk it up with the other players. She just waited her turn to perform and then she put on a show. Offensive coach back then didn't want her to make the team but Coach Sutton could see the talent. After that I'd find her on the field every morning working out. When Coach Sutton finally asked her to step into a game and carry the team, I think I was as proud as her father would've been. She was good when she tried out but she's really good now. If she was a boy, the recruiters would be all over her."

Jamison frowned. "But they aren't?"

"Oh they've been here, but mostly scouting the boys though. I don't think anyone has shown an interest in her." He shook his head. "Best arm in college football."

Jamison could see the confidence that had replaced the cockiness she remembered in the younger Shea. She strolled across the field like she owned it. There was no hesitation when she stepped behind the center and barked out the cadence to put the ball in motion. Silently they watched Shea take snap after snap and run each play like a maestro conducting her own orchestra. It was clear that Shea was the leader on the team and she had earned the respect of the other players. When the players headed back into the tunnel, Jamison was shocked that several hours had passed. She had been drawn into the beauty of Shea's reign over the football field.

Jamison stood and patted Carlton on the shoulder. "Thanks for the company."

"I'm here every day. I never miss a practice."

"Then I'll see you tomorrow," she called over her shoulder. At the stairs she turned back to him. "Cub, huh?"

"Or kitten. She's always been such a sweet thing to me."

Jamison laughed and shook her head. Somehow her impression of Shea didn't match Carlton's. Tiger, maybe, but certainly not kitten.

* * *

Shea hung back from the team, searching the sidelines as she walked toward the tunnel. She hadn't seen Jamison at all while they were on the field and she was beginning to wonder if she had left the stadium. At the edge of the tunnel, she caught a glimpse of Jamison in the stands above her. Shea stopped and watched her maneuver each layer of bleachers. She couldn't pull her eyes from the movement of Jamison's body or stop the smile on her face. She wanted to convince herself she was only waiting for Jamison because that's what she was supposed to do and certainly not because she wanted to.

Dressed in shorts and the blue and black Windbreaker, Jamison looked like a college student but as she came closer, Shea could see the maturity in her face as well as her body. She wasn't overtly feminine in appearance but the Windbreaker did nothing to hide the curve of her breasts and hips. If she was honest, she was beginning to like Jamison's company even more than her attractiveness. Few people had the courage to stand up to her and Jamison had done so from the second they met. She conducted herself with confidence and kindness. Both qualities that made her even more attractive

* * *

Jamison jumped down from the bleachers onto the walkway beside Shea. Together they turned into the tunnel, walking side by side toward the locker room. Jamison glanced at Shea out of the corner of her eye. The edges of her hair were damp from sweat and Jamison resisted the urge to brush the curls back off her neck. She chastised herself for drifting again from being security conscious and forced herself to study the people around them. Her palms began to sweat as she realized how confined they were as they passed through the semidark hallway.

They moved through the men's locker room and into the adjacent hallway. She let Shea lead but stayed close behind her watching in both directions. The athletic trainer Jamison had seen the previous night was coming out of the women's locker room and she held the door open for Shea to enter.

"Ten minutes, Carter. No more. No less," the athletic trainer said as Shea pushed past her.

Shea didn't respond. Jamison looked back and forth between them. The trainer was a little shorter than Jamison and wore the traditional black Tigers shirt with blue trim like all the staff members. She didn't seem bothered by Shea's lack of response. Making eye contact with Jamison, she smiled and then called out to Shea's retreating back. "I'll come check on you in a few."

Jamison took a seat on a stack of floor mats against the rear wall, attempting to blend in with her surroundings. She knew Shea's next actions would involve removing her clothes and she searched for something else to focus on. Shea bent at the waist and pulled her shoulder pads and jersey over her head, tossing them to the floor beside her locker. Her undershirt and shorts joined the growing pile and then she pulled on a long-sleeved T-shirt and sweatpants.

Shea broke the silence. "This is one of the few times you may hear me scream."

Jamison narrowed her eyes as she watched Shea swing her legs into a huge metal tub. Shea's face immediately flushed and her eyes squeezed closed as she lowered her body into the water. Jamison shivered involuntarily when she realized it was an ice bath. Shea hugged her arms across her chest before making eye contact with Jamison.

"If it didn't make me feel so good afterward I'd never go through the agony." Shea dropped her chin to her chest and closed her eyes again.

Jamison watched her start to shiver as the water penetrated her clothing and body. She wondered if football fans really understood what their players went through to be able to perform each week. And this was only college level. She watched Shea breathe deeply and exhale slowly as she attempted to regulate her breathing. For the first time in thirty-six hours, Jamison was able to stare directly at Shea and was surprised to see the dark circles under her eyes. She wondered if Shea had trouble sleeping or if she was more worried about the game than she appeared to be. Her eyes moved down Shea's face to the strong neck as she remembered Shea working out in her sports bra the previous night. Her thoughts torn between the professional she was supposed to be and the woman in front of her, she didn't notice Shea had opened her eyes and was staring back at her.

Shea cleared her throat, her voice quivering as she spoke. "So, what does the security agent think about when on duty?"

Jamison tried to come up with something professional to say. Shea's dark eyes were cloudy with pain and her face was set with determination. She could see that what Shea needed was a distraction and not her rambling, so she said the first thing that came into her mind. "What are the other things that make you scream?"

Shea chuckled but before she could answer the athletic trainer chose that moment to reappear. Jamison hadn't heard the door so she didn't know how long she had been in the locker room with them. Her hope that their conversation hadn't been heard was over when she saw the crooked smile on her face. Thankfully she turned her attention to Shea.

"Nice and refreshing?" she asked.

Shea grimaced.

"Anything more than the usual aches and pains?"

Shea shook her head.

"You're full of conversation today." She glanced at Jamison. "I'm Lynnette, by the way."

Jamison slipped from the mats and stuck out her hand. "Jamison." Lynnette didn't ask who she was and Jamison didn't volunteer. She had to assume the staff had been advised she would be following Shea around but until someone stopped her she wouldn't advertise her position.

Lynnette gave her hand a quick squeeze and returned her attention to Shea. "Do you need me to wrap anything extra before practice tomorrow?"

Shea shook her head. "Just the normal."

"Okay, then I'll see you when you get to the meeting tomorrow." She stepped back and extended a hand. "Let's get you out of there."

"Oh yes," Shea muttered.

Lynnette helped her step out of the tub and handed her a towel. "Hit the shower but not too hot. No need to ruin all the suffering you just did."

Shea disappeared into the shower and Jamison leaned back against the wall to wait.

"How's she handling the security detail?" Lynnette asked as she drained and cleaned the tub.

"We're still working out some kinks," Jamison replied vaguely.

Lynnette smiled knowingly. "She's really sweet except when you want her to do something she doesn't want to do."

"I guess you know her pretty well?"

"They like to throw the two women in a room together when we travel. It has its advantages since she doesn't like to talk about her injuries. Sharing a room helps me get a behind-the-scenes look."

Jamison nodded as Shea came out of the shower wrapped only in a towel.

"I'll see you ladies tomorrow," Lynnette called as she headed toward the door.

Jamison turned her body slightly to watch Lynnette leave and to block her view of Shea. The pink skin displayed around Shea's towel was burned into her mind and she closed her eyes to seal in the vision. Taking a deep breath, she worked through her security checklist, forcing her mind back into protection mode. She needed to be alert as they walked back to the duplex. She couldn't have images of Shea's body breaking her concentration. She felt Shea move beside her and she opened her eyes to find her dressed again. Shea gave her a questioning look before pulling open the door and holding it for Jamison.

They walked down the hallway and out into the humid evening air. Jamison unzipped her jacket, running her hand over her pistol for reassurance. A few students were still moving around the sidewalks but Jamison was learning to identify them from the non-students. Reminding herself that their suspect could be a student made her take a closer look at all the people around them.

Rush hour traffic was over and the few cars on the road moved at a crawl. The farther they moved from campus the fewer students they passed. Everyone seemed to have a destination in mind, either headed home to relax or back to campus for night class.

CHAPTER FIVE

Shea watched Jamison scan the area around them, carefully studying each person that passed. She was tired and had already decided she wasn't going to study tonight. Food was another thought though. She knew there was nothing in her refrigerator.

Jamison touched her arm, giving her a little push, moving them out of the way of a passing student. Shea realized she hadn't even seen the student coming. She glanced around her, making eye contact with Jamison. "There's not much in the house to eat but Pizza Zone has good salads, if you want one."

Jamison studied her face in the early glow of the streetlights. Shea wasn't sure what she saw but Jamison's voice grew soft. "Why don't I fix something? Your body could use something more than lettuce or pizza."

She shrugged. "Sounds good but there's nothing at the house and I don't really feel like going out to get something."

"I picked up some stuff earlier today. I'll make something quick."

She was surprised but pleased. Jamison not only had thought about picking up groceries but had felt her desire to be taken care of. She had never had someone in her life who even asked what she had to eat. When she lived at home her mother had worked a lot of hours and Shea had learned quickly to pick up the phone and order delivery.

* * *

Jamison had expected Shea to refuse the dinner offer but when she accepted she allowed a feeling of anticipation to wash over her. This was her chance to connect with Shea. To make a friend. She also needed to ask her a few questions about the last several weeks and her mind played with how she would casually squeeze them into the conversation. The circles under Shea's eyes and the slow pace they had traveled back to the duplex told her she might have Shea at a disadvantage.

As they climbed the steps to the porch, she dropped back allowing Shea to unlock the door. The motion detector porch light Todd had installed kicked on and she could see the small cameras barely visible in the corners. She smiled. She would have to thank Todd for his excellent work.

"Why the smile?" Shea asked as she held the door open for Jamison.

"Just appreciating the toys my co-workers installed."

Shea frowned. "I didn't think the porch light was on when we turned the corner."

"Motion detection."

"Nice," Shea said as she dumped her backpack on the counter and dropped heavily onto the sofa. "Just five minutes and then I'll help you with dinner."

"Not necessary. I'll let you know when it's ready."

Jamison noticed Shea's eyes were already closed and she wondered if she had even heard her. As quietly as she could she pulled two pots and a pan from the cabinet. She dumped a jar of premade sauce in one pot and filled the other with water. She was anxious to check the cameras so she grabbed her laptop from the guest room and placed it on the counter beside her.

While it booted up, she cut vegetables and tossed them in the skillet with a handful of fresh spinach on top before adding pasta to the boiling water. She opened her email and copied the password Todd had sent her. Logging into the surveillance software she was pleased to see the cameras instantly load.

Four on the front porch and six more strategically placed around the house. Jamison scanned each one carefully, noting their location for quick identification later. The one in the back covered Shea's bedroom window and Jamison was thankful it wasn't there earlier when she had climbed into the house through the window. It would have cost her a lot of money to buy that footage back from Todd.

Happy with the cameras' positioning she closed the laptop confident that Todd would have techs checking footage on a regular basis. She quietly sprinted up the stairs and checked the screen in Shea's bedroom. It was brand new and secure. In the kitchen she put a small amount of pasta on each plate added a larger amount of vegetables and covered it with sauce.

She stepped into the living room but stopped at the corner of the sofa. Shea lay on her left side and her right arm hung off the front of the cushion. Her eyes were closed and her chest rose and fell with her steady breathing. Jamison moved closer and knelt beside her. She couldn't resist brushing a strand of hair back behind Shea's ear before lifting Shea's hand and placing it back on the couch. She slowly ran her fingers across the back of Shea's hand. She smiled at the size difference. She had always felt her hands were large and unlike some women she had never had any difficulty pulling the trigger of her pistol, but her hands were half the size of Shea's.

Before she could consider letting Shea sleep, she began to stir and her eyes slowly opened. A grin spread across her face as she saw Jamison so close to her. Her head tilted a little as she appraised her.

Jamison jumped to her feet. She wasn't sure what Shea had seen when she looked at her.

"Dinner's ready," she said, quickly returning to the kitchen.

Shea stood and stretched, exposing her stomach as her shirt pulled up with the movement of her arms. Her skin was creamy white now, not the pink it had been after the ice bath and she knew it would be soft under her fingers. She took a deep breath and met Shea's gaze. Her dark eyes were darker in the shadows of the room and Jamison caught her breath. She couldn't allow herself to have these feelings for someone she was supposed to protect. She motioned to the table breaking the connection between them.

Shea pulled a bottle of wine from the under the counter. "I don't like to drink alone so this seems like a good time to open this." She reached around Jamison brushing her arm as she grabbed the corkscrew from the drawer.

"Alcohol will dehydrate you," Jamison said softly.

Shea chuckled and opened the bottle, pouring a small amount of wine into each glass and setting them on the table.

Jamison pushed her food around on her plate, unsure she could eat now, her stomach unsettled by thoughts of Shea she couldn't seem to keep at bay. Protection details were hard enough and being on a college campus added an outside dimension she couldn't control. She needed to be on top of her game and not distracted by the tantalizing woman sitting across from her. She looked up to find Shea watching her.

"This is good." Shea held up a forkful of pasta. "Thank you."

"You're welcome." Jamison picked up the wineglass and sniffed. Maybe a little wine would be good for her. She swirled the small amount in her glass and then took a sip. It tasted fruity and the alcohol burned her tongue. She wasn't a drinker and could feel the first sip run all the way to her feet. She needed food or this small glass would make her tipsy. Setting the glass down, she took a bite of pasta and then asked her first question.

"Why football?"

Shea smiled and took a sip of wine. "You can thank my sister for that."

"Mel? What did she do?"

"Oh yes. Mel. When my father died, Mel declared herself the ruler of the house. Mom worked a lot so she wasn't around to rein in the self-appointed king." Shea took another bite. "Did I mention that this is really good?"

"You might have mentioned it." She was pleased to see the short nap had relaxed the circles under Shea's eyes and her face looked less tired. "Continue, please."

"I was about ten and we were watching the Tennessee Titans in the Super Bowl. I'd never watched much football but everyone in town was football crazy since it was the Titans."

"You grew up in Tennessee, right?"

"Yeah, Mom still lives there. Anyway, the game was almost over and during a commercial break, I mentioned there were no women on the field. Mel laughed at me and then said women weren't allowed to play football."

"And those were fighting words?"

Shea grinned. "Pretty much. When the game was over I announced I was going to play football. I harassed my mother until she bought me a football and then I carried it everywhere like it was a doll. I took a lot of taunting from the boys, and some girls, in my class when I informed them I was practicing to play football. When I finally saw the sign for football sign-ups, Mom didn't fight me too much about enrolling. She wasn't happy about it but I think she hoped once I started getting hit I wouldn't want to play anymore."

"But that didn't happen?"

"Hell no. Getting hit made me mad. My first coach was a narrow-minded prick and he didn't want to play me but the boys hadn't begun to grow yet, so I was so much taller. I could catch the ball over their heads and usually I could outrun them. I was entering high school before anyone realized I could throw. Thankfully I never had another coach like my first one. No one discouraged me from playing and my high school coaches even fought the school board to keep me on the team."

Jamison had read some of this in the newspapers but she wanted to hear Shea tell it. "College coaches weren't as encouraging though?" she asked. She was feeling the heady effect of the wine and she also wanted to keep Shea talking so she could gently approach the subject of her current situation.

"No, after high school things fell apart. There were no recruiters calling me and I got angry." Shea shrugged. "It wasn't right and I didn't know how to make a stand so I retreated. The first year after high school I worked as an instructor in a Taekwondo school. Mom thought it would help me learn to control my anger." Shea paused to finish her last bite of pasta.

"I can't imagine what a slap in the face it was to not be recruited."

"No one could imagine a female playing at college level but I couldn't get football out of my head. All I wanted to do was play. Mel convinced me to move to Tallahassee to live with her and I found the local semi-pro women's tackle football team, the Tallahassee Jewels. The coach suggested I help out and not play so I wouldn't hurt my eligibility when I went to college. Between her and Mel, I started to believe in myself again. At first I was just happy to practice with the team but then I started thinking about how I could change people's minds. Turns out all it took was persistence."

"And Coach Sutton."

Shea smiled, drinking the last of her wine. "He's been wonderful," she said as she stood to retrieve the bottle from the counter, pouring more into both their glasses.

"Carlton Hammer says Coach treats you like a princess," Jamison said with an evil grin.

Shea laughed. "Well, I think that's going a bit overboard but hey, I am the star of the team."

Jamison laughed with her. She was surprised at how much they had both relaxed and she accounted for it with the wine. Taking another sip, she asked her first question hoping she wouldn't be met with resistance. "So when did you first hear about the threats to the team?"

The smile on Shea's face dropped and she shook her head. "When I learned they were focused on me. Coach didn't want any of us to worry and I guess no one was really taking any of it seriously at first so he only told the other coaches. We were all a little shook up after the brakes went out on the bus but Coach didn't want us to lose focus so they still didn't tell the team." She sighed, taking several sips of wine before setting her glass a little too hard on the table. "When I was locked in the closet

I thought it was a horrible prank. There are a few guys on the team that I occasionally have issues with and I thought it was them. Coach pulled me in and showed me the note that was left the next day."

Leaning forward in her chair Jamison nodded, and made a mental note to ask Carlton if the players had been looked at as suspects. She wanted Shea's version of events even though she had already read most of what she was saying in the report Carlton had given her. Better if Shea talked without Jamison asking questions. But now there was silence. She studied Shea's face. It held a worried look she hadn't seen before. She didn't want to push Shea too hard but she needed to know her perspective.

"Did you see anything out of the ordinary before you were locked in the closet? A person who shouldn't have been around? Or maybe someone who shouldn't have been near your locker room?"

"I answered those questions to the police already. Didn't you get a copy of the report?"

Jamison nodded, trying to keep her voice gentle. "I did, but I want to hear your observations firsthand."

Shea shrugged. "I didn't notice anything. I was approached from behind and pushed into the closet. I never saw the guy."

"Did you hear the locker room door open or close?"

Shea frowned. "You think he was hiding in the locker room with me?" She shuddered as she said the words. "That's not a pleasant thought."

Jamison touched her hand. "I'm here to keep that from happening."

She watched the worry on Shea's face fade into desire as she looked at Jamison's hand. She quickly tried to pull her hand away but Shea grasped it, wrapping her long fingers gently around Jamison's wrist. Her skin tingled where Shea touched, sending chills through her body.

She closed her eyes as Shea's hand moved to caress her face. She was losing control fast and she struggled to maintain her composure. She took a deep breath and looked into Shea's dark eyes. She was here to protect this woman not seduce her. Though at the moment she wasn't sure who was doing the seducing. Jamison leaned back in her chair, moving out of Shea's reach.

"This is not going to happen, Shea."

Shea smiled. "What's not going to happen?"

"You and me. It's not going to happen. I'm here to do a job."

She saw the quick flash of pain across Shea's face before she jumped to her feet.

"Then just do it."

Shea was gone before she could even think about responding.

* * *

Jamison's words had cut through her. Jamison was here only because she had to be. To do her job. All of the friendliness between them had been a show to get her to be cooperative. Climbing the stairs, she remembered she had left her bag on the kitchen counter. She was certainly not going back to get it tonight. She fell into bed with her clothes on and buried herself in the covers.

It had been years since she had felt anything for a woman. Years since she had even craved the occasional fling. Football was her life and had been for as long as she could remember. She had discovered early on that boys were for playing football and nothing else. Girls were good for experimenting but she couldn't see a relationship with any of them in the near future. She and Mel had talked about her living in the closet but she didn't feel like that was what she was doing. She had her priorities and football was first. Nothing else mattered. Until now. Now that she had connected with Jamison, she finally felt what others talked about. The desire to be close to someone. She wanted to touch Jamison. To feel the softness of her skin beneath her fingertips.

She punched the pillow, taking out her anger. Jamison had rejected her and it hurt. She had seen something in Jamison's eyes before the cutting words had come out of her mouth.

Something she wouldn't be able to easily forget. Something that made her palms sweat and her pulse race. But Jamison had slammed that door closed. If distance was what Jamison wanted, then fine. She would give her distance.

* * *

Jamison leaned her elbows on the table cradling her head. She had given Shea mixed messages and she couldn't blame her for being angry. Maybe this was for the best and could help her keep the barrier between them. Her insides felt cold at the thought of not seeing Shea's smile directed at her. Gathering herself, she got up and carried the plates to the sink. She was here to do a job and she would do it.

Opening the computer she logged into the camera and scanned the area around the house. She needed to find out the camera locations inside the stadium so she sent Carlton an email. She closed the computer and cleaned the kitchen. In the guest bathroom, she found some antibiotic ointment and bandages and doctored her blisters. In bed, at the last minute, she remembered Shea's first class was at ten so she set her alarm for seven to make sure she was up and ready before Shea left the house.

CHAPTER SIX

Jamison slapped the nightstand beside the bed, trying to make the annoying crickets stop chirping. She vaguely remembered setting the alarm tone and at the time the crickets had seemed really cute. Now she only wanted to stomp them. She moaned as she rolled over and cursed the wine she had drunk the night before. It hadn't seemed like much last night but this morning her head was throbbing and her mouth felt fuzzy.

She stumbled to the bathroom and took two aspirin. She was brushing her teeth when she heard Shea descending the stairs. Jamison moved to the bedroom door and listened to her movements in the kitchen. When the front door slammed, she threw her toothbrush in the sink and bolted for the front door.

Shea jogged down the street and disappeared around the corner. Jamison grabbed her pistol and her keys. The weather would probably reach the low eighties today but right now the ground felt freezing on her bare feet. She jumped in her truck and its tires squealed as she gunned the engine. She caught a glimpse of Shea as soon as she turned the corner and eased her foot off the accelerator.

* * *

Shea concentrated on her breathing and the sounds of her footsteps on the pavement. Out of the corner of her eye, she had seen Jamison come out of the house and she knew she would be behind her somewhere. Her mind was still reeling from the words Jamison had said the night before. She had decided this morning if Jamison was only here to do a job then she wouldn't stand in her way nor would she assist her in doing it. Jamison could follow behind her and stay out of her way.

Shea's thoughts drifted to the upcoming game as her lungs sucked in the cool air. Thoughts of the game led to thoughts about the unknown man who was out to get her. Her teammates had teased her and she had laughed it off but who was this guy and how far would he go? She shivered as she realized how vulnerable she was at this very moment. She glanced over her shoulder, scanning the sidewalk behind her for Jamison. She didn't want to admit it but having Jamison around made her feel safer. Her pulse quickened as she discovered there was no sign of Jamison then she caught a glimpse of the dark blue truck moving slowly behind her. She should have known Jamison wouldn't be far behind.

* * *

Jamison saw Shea turn and look behind her. She wanted to believe Shea was looking for her. Apparently she was still upset from her comments the previous night. She wanted to apologize and get back the easy camaraderie that had started to develop between them. She only had to make it until Mel returned and then maybe she could make things right with Shea—if she would let her.

She was relieved when Shea slowed to a walk and returned to the house. She crossed the street and caught the door before Shea could slam it shut. Afraid to take the time for a shower, she quickly pulled on socks and shoes. Shea appeared in time to walk to her class and she left the house without a word. Jamison pulled on the Tigers Windbreaker that she was now beginning to call her own, followed Shea across campus and waited until class started. Returning to the duplex, she showered and dressed in jeans, T-shirt and the Windbreaker. She grabbed her laptop and returned to wait outside Shea's class.

She sat on the floor in the hallway with her computer in her lap. Carlton had sent her a diagram of the inside of the stadium and she tried to memorize the location of the cameras. She was reading through the case file again when she heard the exterior door at the end of the hall slam shut. She looked up making eye contact with a blonde about her own age and height. Her blue eyes were like lasers. Jamison had no doubt that this was TPD Officer Cannon and she quickly rose to her feet. Dressed in jeans and a T-shirt with an open deep green button-down shirt covering a pistol holster either under her arm or in the small of her back. There was no hesitancy in her steps and she scanned the area around her as only a law enforcement officer would.

Jamison moved toward her. "Jamison Krews."

"Heather Cannon."

"Can I get you a drink, Officer Cannon?" Jamison stepped into the alcove leading to the stairs and fed coins into a machine.

"Heather is fine." She nodded toward the machine. "Really?"

Jamison laughed, handing her a small cup, and then fed more coins in for a second cup. "What? It's the best TU has to offer."

Heather took a sip and frowned. "It's more disgusting than I remembered." She looked around her.

Jamison pointed down the hall to the metal trash can.

Heather toasted her with the cup. "Thanks but no thanks."

She covered the distance to the can in three strides and dropped the small cup inside. She leaned against the wall and crossed her arms over her chest. "What can I do for you...and Flagler?"

Jamison took a sip of her coffee giving herself a minute to choose her words carefully. She didn't want to alienate this woman. She needed her cooperation but clearly she was following orders to cooperate with the agent from Flagler.

"I've read the reports but I wanted to get your observations in person."

Heather shrugged. "I wasn't called in until the quarterback was targeted so I haven't had the case very long. Initially patrol officers handled it and unfortunately it was whoever happened to be on duty at the time."

Jamison nodded. "Do you know if there were any cameras in the area where the bus was parked at the hotel?"

"That's the first thing I checked. I tracked the bus from the garage until the team boarded Saturday morning and there was nothing. Though I'm told based on the cut it wouldn't have made it to the hotel so it had to have been done while it was in the hotel parking lot."

"And no cameras?"

"One side of the bus is in view and there was no one hanging around."

Jamison downed the rest of her coffee. "Second cup is better."

Heather grimaced.

"So any leads?"

"Nothing. I've been told the FBI has analyzed the notes but the paper and magazines could have come from any convenience store."

"It feels like we're waiting for him to make the next move and I don't like that."

"'Cause you're the one walking around with the bait?" Heather smiled. "No, I guess that doesn't feel very good. Is she cooperative?"

It was Jamison's turn to shrug. "She has her moments."

Heather handed Jamison her card. "My personal cell number is on it. Use it if you need to reach me and avoid the TPD switchboard."

Jamison pulled a card from her wallet and handed it to Heather. "Please keep me updated."

Heather nodded, giving her a mock salute as she walked away.

Jamison shut down her laptop and placed it back in her bag. She glanced at her watch and realized there would be no lunch again today. Tossing her empty coffee cup in the trash she returned to the vending machine and purchased two granola bars. She consumed one while she waited for Shea to finish her class.

Shea was the first one out of the classroom and her long legs carried her quickly down the hall. Jamison caught up with her as she exited the building. Shea glanced at her but didn't slow down.

"Eat this." Jamison passed her the granola bar.

Shea shook her head. "I don't want that."

"I didn't ask if you wanted it. I just said to eat it." When Shea didn't make any move to take the bar, Jamison continued. "I haven't seen you eat anything all day. You can't keep going at this pace without food."

Shea grabbed the bar, ripped it open and took two quick bites. "Happy now?"

When she nodded, Shea threw the remaining bar in a trash can as they passed.

Jamison shrugged. "Better than nothing."

She saw a hint of a smile cross Shea's face.

They entered the stadium and headed for the locker room. Jamison hung back letting Shea go straight to her locker to prepare for practice. After their talk last night, she wanted to make sure they were alone before she relaxed. Pulling out her pistol, she held it along her leg and out of Shea's view. Slowly she walked around every corner of the locker room and into the showers also checking the supply closet Shea had been locked in. Then she holstered her pistol and returned to her seat in the corner. Shea wore white football pants with a full set of padding but only a black bra. Jamison was surprised to find Shea's dark eyes watching her.

"Are we alone?" Shea asked.

Jamison nodded and her mouth went instantly dry as Shea unhooked her bra, tossing it in her locker and pulling a sports bra over her head. Jamison wrenched her eyes away from the small breasts but not before they were imprinted on her retinas. With a full smile Shea pulled on a skintight sports shirt, tucking it into her pants. She carried her cleats, shoulder pads with jersey and helmet in both hands and headed for the door.

Still stunned by the striptease she had to hurry to catch Shea in the hallway. Inside the men's locker room, Jamison remained near the door with a clear view of Shea but not of the half-dressed men at their lockers. Shea took a seat in front of the whiteboard as she had the previous day and pulled off her socks. Within minutes Lynnette appeared and wrapped both ankles and one of her knees. At exactly two p.m. Coach Sutton stepped out of his office. There was no pep talk today, just straight to business. After a while, the players huddled for a prayer and then moved to the field.

Carlton was sitting in his same spot but before she could join him Coach Sutton sent the offensive line back to the locker room and Jamison followed. She watched Coach Sutton and one of his assistants draw lots of x's and o's all over the board but none of it made sense to her so she watched Shea instead. Shea never lost her concentration or took her eyes off the board. Finally Coach Sutton gestured them to the field and Jamison followed behind the players.

She easily located Carlton again and trotted up the stairs to join him. He acknowledged her arrival with a nod, his attention already focused on the players. She watched the offensive line walk through several of the new plays before lining up opposite the defense.

"Any developments?" Carlton asked.

Jamison shook her head. "Is there ever any security inside the stadium during the week?"

"Not enough manpower. Only the team is allowed in here and we do have cameras at all the entrances."

"And none of the cameras caught anything when the notes were being left?"

Carlton turned to look at her. "Nothing. And I can't figure out how they got in."

Jamison was silent for a while. "Is there a delivery entrance for food and stuff?"

Carlton nodded. "Checked that one too."

"And there is no other entrance?"

Carlton hesitated. "There's a coach's entrance but it has a punch code lock on the door."

"Did you review that camera?"

"I didn't. I just ruled it out since they couldn't get past the locked door."

She frowned. "But maybe he did."

"I'll review them after practice tonight."

"Call me if you see anything, okay?"

He nodded.

Jamison returned her focus to the field as Shea took the ball from center and handed off to her running back. Seconds after the running back was tackled and several of the coaches had blown their whistles, a figure blew past the offensive line and tackled Shea. Jamison could hear the collision from where she was sitting and immediately jumped to her feet. Carlton placed a hand on her arm and pulled her back down but she didn't take her eyes off the field. Several offensive linemen picked up the tackler, tossed him aside and pulled Shea to her feet. Jamison watched her closely and though she was standing on her own she seemed unable to catch her breath.

"That was a hard hit," Jamison said under her breath.

"Yes, it was," Carlton agreed. "And a late one too."

Shea bent over at the waist and placed her hands on her knees. Then she stood straight up and looked at the player who had tackled her.

"Oh she's mad now," Carlton said with a grin.

Though she couldn't hear what the players were saying, Jamison could tell by their actions that they weren't happy with the tackler. They stood in a circle around him and all seemed to be talking at once. When Shea called for them to huddle so she could give them the next play they came reluctantly.

"He's just going to keep playing?" Jamison said indignantly. "No one's going to do anything? What the hell?"

She fought the urge to charge the field and punch the guy herself. Shea might try to appear tough, okay, maybe she was pretty tough, but Jamison had seen her exhausted and vulnerable last night. She couldn't believe Coach Sutton wasn't going to step in and do anything.

Carlton laughed at her consternation. "Don't you worry about my cub. He'll get what's comin' to him. You might not see it but those guys that protect her will take care of him."

Jamison watched Shea take her position behind center and call the cadence. When the ball moved it seemed almost in slow motion. The offensive line parted and Shea threw a bullet into the tackler's crotch. He collapsed onto the ground rolling back and forth until his teammates pulled him to his feet. Shea called her next huddle and the offense took the line quickly giving him no time for recovery.

Jamison stared in wonder but Carlton chuckled softly beside her. "Shouldn't piss her off."

"No, I guess not." Jamison relaxed back into her seat. She was impressed with the way Shea handled the situation, realizing that this was probably not the first time Shea had dealt with unruly team members. "Was a check run on the players too?"

Carlton grunted. "I was told that was too invasive when I suggested it to the police officer so I did a search myself. Coach and I are pretty confident we cleared them all."

She nodded. "Do you know anything about the kid that just hit her?"

"An aggressive sophomore trying to win a place on the first string. I don't think it's anything more than that and I don't think he'll make a late hit again."

She stood as the players started to leave the field. "Tomorrow, then."

Carlton gave her a nod.

Like yesterday, Shea waited at the edge of the tunnel for her to climb down the bleachers and then they walked together in silence. She wanted to say something about the late tackle but wasn't sure how to word it and she didn't want to disrupt the amicable silence they were developing again. She glanced at Shea out of the corner of her eye and found her looking back.

Shea grinned. "I'm okay."

Jamison nodded. That was all she needed to know.

"The weight room is going to be pretty smelly today with all the guys in there but I'll work through my set as quick as I can."

Jamison nodded again.

"I'm going to dinner with some of the guys after practice," Shea said reluctantly.

"I'll stay out of sight. Is it within walking distance or will I need my truck?"

"We can walk. Mike's on Tennessee Street. It's a burger place."

Jamison grimaced and Shea laughed. "They serve other stuff too but we go there for the burgers."

CHAPTER SEVEN

Shea groaned as she pushed the bar over her head again. This was her last set and she was hoping to escape without an ice bath tonight. Lynnette seemed to be busy with the guys and hadn't mentioned it to her. As if Lynnette had heard her thoughts, Shea saw her turn in her direction so she closed her eyes to concentrate on the weight.

"Your bath is set." Shea heard a soft whisper in her ear. "And don't bother getting fully dressed after your shower, I want to see those ribs."

"Crap," Shea said as Lynnette walked away.

Josh, her center and pretty much favorite guy on the team, laughed softly. "Ice bath?"

"Yes, dammit."

"She takes such good care of you," he teased.

She rolled her eyes. Finished with her last set she sat up on the bench and scanned the room. Her eyes met Jamison's and held for a moment.

"She your bodyguard or girlfriend?" Josh asked, his voice still teasing.

She narrowed her eyes. "What's it to you?"

"I was thinking about asking her out that's all. She's kinda hot." Josh stood and pushed her off the bench. "You're done here, right?"

Shea considered punching him. She knew he was only kidding but her jealousy had flared instantly. Jamison *was* hot. She involuntarily glanced in her direction again. Wearing jeans and Shea's Tigers Windbreaker, Jamison looked relaxed and not really out of place in the Tigers team weight room.

Shea liked the way Jamison never seemed to get ruffled even when she gave her a reason to be angry. Her own childhood had always been a constant state of turmoil. Her mother was either angry or excited, there was never a downtime and Mel was the same way until she moved out of the house. It took Mel years to become the solid person emotionally that she was now. Shea struggled to find an even keel. Football had helped but still some things disrupted her emotions, like the arrival of Jamison.

She was ready to leave football and everything that went with it behind her for the night but she had already agreed to dinner.

Josh was watching her closely. "You know I was just kidding about asking her out, right? She is hot and all but I can see you guys got a connection. I wouldn't do anything to screw that up for you."

She grinned at him. "Shut up, Josh, before I punch you."

He laughed. His happy demeanor returned, his attention went back to lifting weights. For a minute, she watched the muscles in his biceps bulge as he pushed the weight bar over his head. She was thankful to have him for her protection on the field. All of the guys on her offensive line were beefy with plenty of muscle strength too. She'd been sacked only twice this year because these guys took their job seriously and didn't mess around where her safety was concerned. Maybe it was because she was a female but really she didn't care why. Whatever it took to make them strive to protect her was not important—only that they did.

She headed for the door without looking behind her. She could feel Jamison's presence. When they returned to the women's locker room, she watched Jamison again search every corner, her pistol casually at her side. She tried to ignore the uneasiness she felt at the idea someone could be waiting to harm her. When Jamison relaxed, taking her usual seat on the stack of mats, she wasted no time returning her focus to getting out of there for the night.

She quickly switched into long sleeves and sweats before climbing into the ice bath. She was reminded of the earlier hit when she lifted her arms above her head, stretching her rib cage. She had thought no one had noticed when she skipped the weight machines that would put the most strain on that area of her body, but now she wondered if maybe Lynnette had noticed. She gently lowered herself into the freezing water, trying to clear her head and focus on something other than the ice. After a few minutes, she settled back against the tub making sure her throwing arm was completely submerged.

"Does it burn?"

Shea looked up to find Jamison watching her. "No, unless it touches my skin. It's more of a mind-numbing pain. The initial shock is the worst then it just settles into a dull ache."

"But it makes you feel better?"

"Oh yeah. That's why you don't see any of us complain about it too much."

They both turned as the locker room door opened and Lynnette appeared. "How bad was the hit? One to ten?"

She groaned. Lynnette always asked that and then she never believed the answer. "Not more than a five. He really just knocked the wind out of me."

Lynnette rolled her eyes. "Save it, Carter. You skipped two machines in the weight room so hit the shower and I'll draw my own conclusions."

With Lynnette's help, she climbed out of the tub and stepped into the showers.

Lynnette asked Jamison quietly, "Have there been any developments?"

Shea had wanted to ask the same question but she knew it wouldn't be answered truthfully.

"I'm not really working on the case. I'm just here to make sure he…or she isn't able to reach Ms. Carter again."

If Lynnette responded, Shea didn't hear her. She dressed quickly in a sports bra and underwear before allowing Lynnette to begin her evaluation. She couldn't stop the occasional grimace when Lynnette zeroed in on a bruised area.

"Nothing is broken. Some serious bruising though." She crossed the room to the office and returned with an arm full of bandages. "Let's wrap it for the next couple of days. You know the drill. Contact me immediately if the pain intensifies or you have trouble breathing."

She stood quietly while Lynnette wrapped her ribs and then she dressed quickly. Jamison followed her out of the locker room and across the darkening campus.

"I don't plan on staying long," she told her as Mike's came into view. "I have some stuff to work on tonight but I'd already agreed to come along."

"That's fine. I'll follow you out whenever you're ready."

* * *

College students filled every available space and they all seemed eager to talk with Shea. Jamison remained near the door waiting to see where Shea would settle. Shea chose a table near the far wall already crowded with several men and one woman. Jamison moved to a booth in the corner and slid in giving herself a clear view of Shea. The waitress approached quickly and Jamison ordered a grilled chicken salad with spinach. She was scanning the room when her phone vibrated. She swiped to accept the call when she saw Heather's name.

"News?" Jamison asked as her greeting.

"Maybe. Narcotics picked up a guy with a stash of cocaine. He wants to negotiate and says he has information on the bus tampering. I'm just arriving at the station now so I'll call you back after I talk with him."

"Sounds good." Jamison punched her phone off. Heather was all business and Jamison liked that about her. She had originally thought she would have her hands in the investigation too but after meeting Heather this morning she no longer felt that was necessary. Heather had proved her right by not waiting or hesitating to fill her in.

Jamison went back to scanning the customers and the waitstaff. No one seemed to be focused on Shea more than normal. She noticed Shea was watching her. Jamison allowed her eyes to lock with Shea's. She struggled to read the dark eyes burning into her own. From across the room it was hard to tell the exact color and she had already learned that was the only way she knew to read Shea. Her eyes were a creamy dark until she got angry and then the color deepened. Jamison's body gave an involuntary shudder as she thought about the dark arousal she had seen in Shea's eyes the night before. Again she wondered if there would be anything left of their relationship when this case was over. She couldn't open that door by asking Shea to wait until then. Best for Shea to think there was no opportunity for anything between them so Jamison could focus entirely on the case. Her eyes caught Shea's again as a grin slid across her face. What had Shea seen in her face to make that grin appear? She was glad the waitress chose that moment to arrive with her salad.

Jamison's phone buzzed as she was taking her last bite and she immediately picked up Heather's call.

"How'd it go?"

"He was a fountain of rambling but I might've gotten something. He identified the make and model of a car that was idling near the bus. A white Honda Accord in the old box style. Probably a late nineties model."

"That's something. Anything on the person?"

"Nothing specific. Dark clothes with a hood up. I'm going through surveillance at the hotel again. Maybe I'll catch a glimpse of him or the car. One of the other guys is pulling all the older white Honda Accord registrations within a sixty-mile radius. I'll email you the records when I get them. It looked like about ten or so."

"I'll contact Carlton Hammer with Tallahassee University security and have him pull the tapes and see if we can spot the car around campus."

"Okay. Let me know if you guys turn up anything on your end."

It was almost nine p.m. Out of the corner of her eye, Jamison caught a glimpse of Shea standing beside her table so she quickly paid her bill, crossed to the exit and waited outside for Shea. They walked together down the sidewalk and headed back toward campus. The traffic on the street was light and there weren't many people hanging around.

Jamison wanted to ask how she was feeling but knew Shea wouldn't respond well to that question. Shea wanted to belittle the situation and Jamison needed to honor her feelings. So, instead she asked about dinner.

"How was your burger?"

"Greasy. And your salad?"

"Not greasy."

Shea led the way into the duplex, disappearing upstairs. Jamison logged onto the security cameras and scanned the footage from around the house while they had been gone, then brought up her email. Heather had sent copies of the driver's licenses for the owners of all ten Honda Accords and she forwarded them on to Todd, requesting that he have a tech run background checks on each person. She considered calling Carlton to ask about the surveillance tapes but it was late so she sent him an email too. There had been no movement upstairs in over an hour so she went to bed as well.

CHAPTER EIGHT

Wednesday morning, Jamison checked the street and then stood aside for Shea to exit. At Shea's first class Jamison took her usual seat in the hallway with her laptop. She had received reports back from the tech center and managed to go through all ten backgrounds by the time Shea departed her classroom an hour later. She had arranged the files in order of potential suspects, even though none of them had any prior police records, and emailed the file to Carlton. After she dropped Shea at her second class of the day, Jamison crossed campus to the security office and located Carlton.

"Good morning," he greeted her as soon as she walked through the door. "I've been scanning the files you sent but I haven't finished yet. Anyone stand out to you?"

"Unfortunately no, but at least we know what he might've been driving. Can you pull up the surveillance tapes and see if you can match the vehicle?"

"My secretary's pulling all the tapes for those days."

"Email me some of the files and I'll have the techs at Flagler work on it too."

She could tell he wanted to do the work himself but he reluctantly nodded. "I'll see how much I can get through in the next hour or so and then I'll split the rest with you."

She dialed Flagler and waited for Todd to pick up as she walked back to Shea's classroom. "Are you having the footage from my cameras watched every day?"

"Yes, but unfortunately it's the night shift. I have it running live on the monitor beside me but I haven't been able to watch it consistently."

"I understand. I know you have other work too. At least if someone is scanning it each night they'll catch someone hanging around."

"They'll be long gone," Todd said with regret.

"But we might get a visual on a face and that would help." She saw Shea step out of the building with her lunch friend from Monday and two other guys. Jamison recognized them all from the dinner group last night. She fell into step behind them. "Thanks for all your help, Todd. I better run."

Jamison considered calling Mel with an update but really they didn't have much yet. They were finally chasing a lead and that, at least, felt good. She was surprised when Shea held the sub shop door open for her and then motioned for her to join their table.

"I'm Mindi. This is my boyfriend, Doug, and that's Josh."

"Jamison."

She ate quietly as the conversation went from classes to football.

"Have you been to a game?' Mindi asked her.

"Never in person but I watch on television."

"Did you watch last weekend?" Doug asked. "It was a great game."

Jamison replayed the game in her mind, looking for a moment that stood out. "I did. It was a good game. I was scared for a short time toward the end when they scored and then almost scored again."

Josh jumped into the conversation. "Right. Our defense lost their minds and allowed them to walk right down to the twenty. Luckily Harper got that interception."

"That wasn't luck, man. We were still up by a touchdown. That game was in the bag," Doug said.

"This is the last regular season game, right?" Jamison asked, even though she knew the answer. "Jacksonville?"

"Right," Josh answered. "And this year we have Shea so they don't stand a chance."

Shea stood. "At the risk of counting our chickens before they've hatched, I'm going to class."

Jamison stepped onto the sidewalk and held the door for Shea.

"I didn't realize you were a football fan," Shea said as they approached the campus.

"I like to watch on my free weekends. And yes, I do watch Tallahassee."

Shea grinned. "I'll see you in an hour?"

She nodded, taking a seat on the floor beside her computer bag.

* * *

Jamison leaned back in the stadium chair and enjoyed what had quickly become her favorite part of the day. She and Carlton watched the team run through play after play while they sat in the late afternoon sun. She watched Shea run the ball on a quarterback sneak play. She seemed much more relaxed than Jamison had seen her all week. Even the team seemed to have an easygoing attitude. It must have been a good practice because Coach Sutton released them about thirty minutes early.

Shea waited for her at the edge of the tunnel as she had the last two days and they walked together to the weight room. She watched Shea move through her workout and was surprised to find her ready to go as soon as she finished.

"No ice bath tonight?" she asked as they exited the locker room.

"I talked Lynnette out of it. I want to go home, shower and lay on my couch."

Jamison laughed. "That sounds like a good plan."

Shea strode down the hall and stopped in front of a wall filled with boxes. "Team mailboxes," she explained. "Seldom anything important but sometimes Lynnette will put supplies we ask for in there." She tossed a small box into her backpack. "Like my new mouth guard."

As they left the stadium, Shea began her plea for pizza. Jamison let her argue her case and then simply said no. Their banter was friendly and filled with laughter.

"But Jimmy's going to think I don't like him anymore," Shea pretended to whine.

"You just had pizza on Sunday. I'll bake chicken."

"If you must," Shea surrendered. "What'll you make with it, Chef Krews?"

"Lots of vegetables," Jamison teased.

"That's terrible," Shea groaned, depositing her backpack beside the couch. "I'm going to shower."

Jamison turned the oven on to preheat and placed the raw chicken breast into a baking dish, covering it with Italian dressing. She laid out some vegetables, chopped them up and added them to a bowl of lettuce and spinach. She moved to grab her laptop and met Shea at the foot of the stairs.

"I'm going—" Jamison started.

"No, I don't think you are."

Shea grasped her by the waist and pushed her onto the couch, straddling Jamison's lap. Their faces were close and she stared into the dark eyes unable to look away. What would one kiss hurt? Just one. Shea's skin was cool from her shower and the lavender smell was intoxicating.

* * *

Shea watched the range of emotions cross Jamison's face. She hadn't planned this but now she couldn't stop. The flames of desire had engulfed her and Jamison's expression mirrored her own. She gently tilted Jamison's chin. She knew any second Jamison would come to her senses and she would quickly be dismissed. Slowly, she touched her lips to Jamison's and held them there. Her tongue softly played along Jamison's lips, patiently waiting until Jamison's tongue met hers and the kiss deepened. She couldn't hold back any longer and she pushed deeper into Jamison's mouth. She felt Jamison surrender for barely a second and then the timer went off on the stove.

Jamison broke the kiss and slid Shea off her lap, jumping to her feet. "Dammit, Shea. I can't...You can't." Her frustration clearly visible, she disappeared into the kitchen.

"I think we just did," Shea said to the empty room.

CHAPTER NINE

Jamison slapped the oven timer to stop the beeping and leaned against the counter trying to get control of her body. The look of desire she had seen on Shea's face before she had closed her eyes had unnerved her. Her own emotions had been reflected back at her and she wanted to give into them. She crossed her arms over her chest and took several deep breaths. She needed to walk into the living room and give Shea a firm no, but she couldn't even form a full sentence in her head let alone make words come out of her mouth. At this moment, she wouldn't be very convincing.

She took a quick look in the living room as she retrieved her laptop. Shea was lying on the couch with the remote on her chest but her eyes watched Jamison walking past. She shuddered and hoped that Shea hadn't noticed the effect her eyes had on her. She couldn't even think about the rest of Shea's body but her mind could. In fact, her mind couldn't stop.

She booted up her computer and pulled up the surveillance cameras, checking first the live feeds before scrolling through today's recordings. The television was muted but movement from a football game on the screen caught her attention. A quarterback rolled out of the pocket and as he pulled back to throw the defense slammed him hard to the ground. She spoke without thinking. "That was stupid. He moved out of the pocket when he would've been safe there."

Shea's head appeared over the top of the couch. "That was a correct observation, Coach Krews."

She rolled her eyes and returned her gaze to the camera footage. She could feel Shea's eyes still on her.

"I wasn't being sarcastic, Jamison. You were correct and I won't make the same mistake. Their defense is killer and if I move out of the protection of my offensive line, they'll get me every time. Come watch with me," Shea suggested.

She glanced at her computer screen. She would rather be with Shea analyzing the football game. She closed her laptop and took a seat in the living room chair out of touching distance. A box on the floor in front of Shea's open backpack caught her eye. "Shea, what did you say was in that box?"

"My new mouth guard. I'll wear it tonight while I sleep to get used to it."

"Was it shipped from somewhere or did Lynnette pick it up?" Jamison asked, still studying the box.

Shea shrugged. "I guess Lynnette picked it up. I really don't know."

"Do your supplies normally come like that?" Jamison looked at her.

"What do you mean?" Shea started to reach for the box.

"No!" Jamison put her hand out to stop Shea. "There's no return address but your name and address are written out fully. It's like it came through the mail."

Shea frowned. "I don't know."

"Do you have a number for Lynnette? Can you call her?"

Shea nodded and reached for her cell phone.

"Wait. Let's step out on the porch."

Shea was puzzled but she followed Jamison out of the house.

"Lynnette, its Shea. I'm sorry to bother you."

Jamison listened while they exchanged greetings, her eyes locked on Shea's.

"Did my mouth guard come in yet…No, it's fine. You said when you ordered it that it might not come in before the game."

Jamison had heard enough. She dialed Flagler and asked for Bowden. Thankful that Mel had given her a point of contact for assistance.

Shea was still talking with Lynnette and Jamison looked up at her when she asked, "Did you put something else in my team box?" She shook her head at Jamison.

"Oh, yes, Agent Krews. I'll put you right through to Mrs. Bowden," the Flagler technician said.

While she waited on the line, she took Shea by the hand and walked her across the street to her truck. She motioned for Shea to climb in. Closing the door behind her, Jamison paced on the sidewalk.

"Jamison? What's wrong?" Bowden asked.

"Ms. Carter received a package in her team mailbox today. She thought it was something she was expecting. I didn't become suspicious until I saw the writing on the outside. It was fully addressed with her information but no return address. We have confirmed it is not the package Ms. Carter was expecting."

"Okay. I've heard enough. Are you out of the house?"

"Yes, we're across the street in my truck."

"I'll have someone there shortly."

The dial tone buzzed in her ear.

She climbed into the truck and gave Shea a small smile. "How about some pizza?"

While Shea called in the order, Jamison considered calling Heather but if it turned out to be nothing she was going to feel like an idiot. Same thing with Mel and Carlton. She would fill everyone in once she knew whether there was anything to tell them. She looked up to find Shea watching her. Her face was creased with worry.

"You think it's a bomb?" Shea asked softly.

"I think we should be safe and not take any chances."

"What's going to happen now?"

Jamison smiled, trying to lighten Shea's mood. "One of two things. The bomb squad will show up and clear the package."

"Or?"

"The house will blow up and we won't need the bomb squad."

Shea chuckled. "That's nice, Jamison."

Jamison stared out her window at the duplex. "How long has it been empty?" She motioned toward the other half of Shea's building.

"About a month. He was evicted. I wasn't sorry to see him go. He had a dog that barked all the time and I think it chewed on most of the fixtures in the house. I was home the day the landlord came to check it out and he said he probably wouldn't be able to rent it again until next fall."

"Why so long?" Jamison wanted to keep Shea talking so she wasn't thinking about their situation.

"He won't do repairs until summer. He does everything himself and he travels in the winter. He's a friend of Coach Sutton so I just go to him if I need something but really it's been great. No plumbing or heating issues. The guy does good work so it's not like most rentals."

A black SUV pulled into the space in front of Jamison's truck. She climbed out, telling Shea, "Please, stay in the truck."

Shea nodded.

"Agent Krews?" the driver asked as he extended his hand. "I'm Sam."

"Sorry to call you guys out this evening."

"Not a problem. We always enjoy a good suspicious package." Tall and muscular, he smiled down at her. "You can watch the monitor with me, if you want."

He stepped to the rear of the SUV and opened the hatch. Computer equipment and a monitor screen were permanently mounted to the vehicle.

"John Sully will control Alpha's movements from inside the response van."

He motioned to a black van pulling to a stop directly in front of the duplex. Two young men jumped out. The shorter one with red hair removed a robot, presumably Alpha, from the inside of the van and the other climbed inside the rear of the van.

"House unlocked?" Sam asked.

She nodded.

"You're clear, Sully," Sam called to the man with the robot.

Sully set the robot on the sidewalk and climbed into the rear of the response van.

Jamison watched the robot on adjustable legs climb the stairs of the duplex and reach up, opening the front door. She couldn't help but smile and turned to see if Shea was watching too. Shea's gaze was locked on the robot now disappearing inside the house.

"Do you mind if Ms. Carter joins us?" Jamison asked Sam.

"Will she have a problem if we have to blow it in place?"

Jamison motioned for Shea to get out of the truck. "She won't be happy but she'll understand."

Jamison saw the flicker of recognition on Sam's face when Shea approached them. "Shea, this is Sam. Sam, Shea." He shook her hand quickly and then returned to his monitor. "I'm a fan, Ms. Carter. Big fan. It's nice to meet you."

"And you too, Sam. Thanks for helping us out here." Shea shrugged at Jamison. "It's a football town."

"You are correct on that," Sam said, his focus still on the monitor. "Sully's finished with his preliminary testing. Where's the package located?"

"The living room floor," Jamison answered.

She watched the monitor as Alpha moved slowly through the kitchen and into the living room. The package came into view.

"I don't see any wires on first pass." Sam punched a few buttons, picking up the feed from the response van. "There's no radiation, so that's good."

An interior view of the package displayed on the screen. "Nope, definitely no wires. That's real good. Sully, what's that black spot on the right?" He paused while he listened. "Okay. Sounds good." He turned back to Jamison and Shea. "We think the black spot…" He pointed at the monitor. "Right here, is a blasting cap."

Shea gasped and then quickly placed a hand over her mouth. Jamison put an arm around her waist and gave her a squeeze while Sam continued. "We don't see any wires or timers though, so Sully's going to move in for a visual and confirm that."

"He's going into the house?" Shea asked in surprise.

As if on cue, Sully stepped out of the van and trotted up the steps into the house. Sam nodded. "We're confident about what we're seeing or I wouldn't allow him to do that. We have other options. Alpha can cover the box with a bomb plate and we can detonate on the spot but I don't think that's necessary."

They watched Sully's hands through Alpha's monitor as he opened the box. He pulled a folded up letter out first and then an old-fashioned Polaroid photo.

Sam spoke into his microphone. "Yes, bring it all out."

The video began to wobble as Sully picked up Alpha to carry it out of the house. Sam shut off the monitor and closed the hatch of his SUV.

"All clear, ladies. If it's okay with you I'll hang until TPD gets here. Sully will burn the footage of what we just did to a disk and they'll want that as well as a report from me." He passed Jamison a pair of gloves. "Probably no prints but just in case." He pulled on a pair of his own.

Sully handed Sam the box, nodded and crossed back across the road, disappearing into the van with Alpha still in his arms.

Sam pulled the Polaroid out first.

Jamison stared at the photo of her and Shea walking on campus.

"That's us," Shea gasped.

Sam dropped the photo back in the box and handed Jamison the letter. She opened it carefully holding it by the edges, making sure nothing fell out. Pasted on letters covered the paper and she read aloud.

"Boom! It would have been that easy. You and your NEW friend would both be gone. See you Saturday."

She felt Shea shiver beside her and she gave her arm a quick squeeze. She dropped the letter and envelope into the evidence bag Sam held. Pulling her phone from her pocket, she dialed Heather and quickly explained the situation.

"TPD is on the way," Jamison said, disconnecting, though as usual Heather was already gone.

Sam nodded. "Let's get off the street."

"Pizza's here," Shea said.

Jamison met the driver at the car and paid him, taking the pizza and drinks into the house. Sam and Shea followed her. She passed around bottles of water then joined them at the table. Shea pulled two pieces of pizza onto a paper plate and went into the living room. She sat in the chair, giving herself a view of the table, but she hit play on the DVD player to start the game footage again.

"Will you let Mrs. Bowden know the outcome? I hate to call her again at home," Jamison asked.

"I sent her a text when we were all clear and she'll call one of us if she wants more details before morning."

Jamison lowered her voice. She knew Shea was listening to the conversation though her gaze was focused on the television screen. "Were the explosives real?"

Sam appeared to contemplate what he wanted to say. "I think so but we'll let the lab guys say for sure. If they are, they should be able to track the origin." He took another bite of pizza. "The FBI will probably want all of the evidence but you might convince them to give you a copy of the note."

"I'll let TPD handle that fight."

Jamison left the room and returned with her laptop bag. She pulled two incident report forms from her bag and passed one to Sam. Silently they both documented their part in finding the evidence. Sam finished first and taking another slice of pizza he joined Shea in front of the television.

Jamison sent a short text to Mel letting her know everything was okay in case she heard the bomb squad was called out through other Flagler channels. She saw movement on the porch as the motion light kicked on.

Heather tapped lightly on the door and Jamison held it open allowing her and a man in a black suit inside.

Heather motioned at him. "FBI Special Agent Andrew Wallace."

Jamison shook his hand. "Jamison Krews."

While Andrew and Sam exchanged greetings, Heather shrugged at Jamison. "I had to call him," she said softly.

"I understand. Pizza?" She motioned at the table.

Heather shook her head. "No thanks." She turned to where the two guys were going through the evidence bag. She frowned at Jamison when she saw the picture. "Sitting ducks is right. I'll make you a copy of the picture and the note when Agent Wallace sends one to us."

Wallace nodded. "I want to get this to the lab as soon as possible but I'll have them make copies." He nodded at Heather. "Thanks for calling me. I'll be in touch."

They watched the door close behind him before anyone spoke.

"I'll be in touch my ass," Heather mumbled.

Jamison and Sam laughed.

"I'll email Mr. Personality a copy of our incident reports and footage from the package retrieval." He nodded to Jamison. "I'll copy you on it."

"And I'll forward it to you," Jamison said to Heather.

"Not tonight though." Sam smiled. "I'm headed home now. Nice meeting you, Ms. Carter. Good luck on Saturday."

"Thank you," Shea called from the living room.

"Thanks, Sam." Jamison shook his hand.

"No problem. Happy to help."

As the door closed behind Sam, Heather spoke. "The note is probably worthless again but maybe the FBI will get something from the explosives."

Jamison glanced at Shea and lowered her voice. "That would certainly help. Any luck with the car?"

"We interviewed all of the owners today. Each was able to account for where they were during the time the brakes were tampered with."

"Maybe someone borrowed the car? Family member? Friend?"

"It doesn't appear so. I'm afraid we might have a car without registration."

"Another dead end. I thought the low number of matching vehicles gave us better odds." Jamison rubbed her face. "I can't believe he was so close and I didn't see him."

Heather frowned. "How could you? You don't know who you're looking for. It's not like he's wearing a sign."

"He was using a fucking Polaroid camera, not a zoom lens—which means he was too close for me to miss him."

"Right, in a crowd of college students."

Jamison shrugged. "Maybe. But I still need to get on top of this before he gets any closer. He has something planned for the game on Saturday so we need to catch him now."

Heather nodded. "I agree. I pulled traffic camera footage from around the hotel. Maybe I'll get a shot of the car coming or going and a view of his license plate."

"I'll check with the techs at Flagler and see if they've spotted the car around the stadium when the notes were left." Jamison's phone buzzed and she glanced at the caller ID. "Crap." She nodded toward the living room. "Her sister."

Heather grimaced and turned toward the door. "I've got reports to write."

Jamison secured the deadbolt behind Heather as she swiped to accept Mel's call. "Hey Carter."

"What's going on James?"

"He put a package in her team mailbox. She thought it was her new mouth guard left by the athletic trainer and carried it home. Flagler sent a bomb squad—"

"Yeah, I heard that."

She sighed. "Which is why I sent you the text earlier."

"And I did appreciate it especially since I wasn't able to call until now. So what was in the box?"

"Explosives. But no wires connecting the blasting cap and no trigger or timer." She hesitated. "And a note."

She hated to tell Mel she had fucked up but knew she didn't have a choice. Jamison recited aloud the words from the note, which were now burned into her mind. "There was also a Polaroid picture."

"A Polaroid. What the fuck?" Mel exploded.

"Shea and I walking together on campus."

"Could you tell where you were located on campus? Maybe you could pin him down to an area."

"Unfortunately the picture was too close to see much of anything around us. FBI took the original but claim they'll send us copies."

"Really? That close, huh?" Mel hadn't missed Jamison's words.

"Yeah, too damn close." She listened to the silence on the other end for a few seconds. "I'm sorry, Mel. I won't let it happen again."

Mel sighed. "I know you're doing the best job possible. It's hard because I want to be there. Just keep me in the loop. We're still hoping to wrap this up and be out of here on Friday."

"I'm working closely with TPD and they're following a few leads so hopefully something will hit soon."

She disconnected the call. She needed a game plan. She turned to grab her laptop and found Shea leaning against the kitchen table. How much of the conversation with Mel had she heard?

"That was my sister?"

"It was. She's still hoping to be back by Saturday."

Jamison stepped around her and picked up her laptop. Flipping open the screen she sat down at the table. She logged into the camera surveillance from around the house and began reviewing the footage from earlier.

"You can't blame yourself for not seeing him. I was with you too." Shea sat down beside her.

Jamison was silent. Surely Shea didn't believe that. This was her profession. Of course she should have seen someone that close to them taking pictures.

Shea touched her arm. "Jamison."

Taking a deep breath, she finally looked at her. Shea's face was etched with concern and she wasn't sure if it was for her or their situation.

"I haven't taken any of this seriously but I will now. I'll do whatever you tell me and I won't try to do anything on my own."

Jamison nodded. "Okay."

Shea's touch turned into a caress as she lightly stroked Jamison's arm. Jamison stared into her eyes wishing this were another time or another place and that there wasn't a crazed lunatic following them around. Shea tucked a strand of hair behind Jamison's ear, stroking her cheek and then slid her hand behind Jamison's neck. Gently she pulled Jamison's face toward her.

Jamison removed Shea's hand from her neck and placed it back on the table. She turned her attention to the laptop. "I need to review this camera footage."

With resignation, Shea stood. "I'd like to go for a run in the morning."

"I'll be ready by seven."

Shea turned and disappeared up the stairs.

Jamison dropped her face in both hands. She had no choice. Her priority needed to be Shea's safety and she couldn't do that if all she could think about was the softness of her skin. She picked up her cell phone and dialed Flagler while she pulled up the camera locations inside the stadium. Time to concentrate on finding this lunatic. Of course there was only one camera in that area but it faced the elevator. Nothing on the team boxes or the stairs.

Jamison recognized the female voice from previous calls to Flagler. "This is Jamison Krews. I sent some camera footage to be reviewed and I was wondering if there was a status."

"Right, Todd's case. Hang on a second and I'll get him."

Jamison frowned as elevator music played in her ear. She hadn't expected Todd to be working this late.

"Hey Krews." Todd's voice came on the line sounding chipper for the late hour.

"What are you doing in the office now?"

"Working, working, working," Todd continued without giving her a chance to respond. "We've reviewed all of the footage and we didn't catch a glimpse of his car."

"I was afraid of that. He was probably on foot when he approached the stadium. Easier to blend in as a student."

"I was thinking the same thing." Todd paused. "Which is why I'm designing a program to look for duplicate faces. I should have it up and running by morning. I talked with Mr. Hammer on campus and he gave me access to the student ID database so I'll be able to identify students."

"Wow. That's some positive news. I needed that tonight. Thanks, Todd."

"No problem. I'd been thinking about writing this program anyway and now I have a reason to. I'll let you know when I find something."

Jamison returned to her review of the camera footage. There wasn't a lot, since foot traffic near the house was light. She watched Shea leaning on the porch railing as she talked to Lynnette on the phone earlier and she studied her face. She could see the concern and maybe a little fear as she realized Lynnette had not placed the package in her box. Movement over Shea's shoulder caught Jamison's eye. She tried to zoom in but everything out of the porch light range was fuzzy. It looked like a person and she grabbed her phone again. This time when the female voice answered she didn't identify herself. "I need to talk with Todd."

"Sure."

Todd came instantly on the line. "Krews?"

"Todd, have you looked at the footage from the house cameras today yet?"

"No, I've been working on the program. Techs are going through it though."

"Skip to seven twenty-six. It looks like someone is standing in the shadows behind Shea."

"Doing it now. Give me a second." She could hear Todd punching keys and muttering to himself. "Okay. I see it. I'll try to blow it up and make it clearer but it's going to take some time."

"Call me back."

He repeated, "It's going to take some time, Krews. Go to bed and I'll talk with you in the morning."

She sighed. "Okay."

She stared at the computer screen. *Could he really be this stupid?* Maybe this was the break they had been hoping for. She closed her laptop and went to bed.

CHAPTER TEN

Jamison was sitting at the kitchen table in the muted light from the hood above the stove when Shea came downstairs. Shea watched her wince as she gently pulled thick socks over bandages covering both heels. She knew the pain that blisters caused and wondered if she was responsible. Of course she was. She had been nothing but difficult since the day Jamison arrived and she would cancel this run if it would alleviate Jamison's pain. Knowing Jamison's determination though, she couldn't let her know why she wanted to change her plans and unfortunately it was too late to come up with a believable excuse.

In silence, she walked to the door and waited for Jamison to clear their exit. The sky was barely starting to glow with the morning sun. The day was cool but the sun would bring warmth and humidity within the hour. She watched Jamison pull the bottom of her sweatshirt over the pack at her waist. She knew Jamison wasn't the queen of style but she wouldn't wear something that unsightly unless there was a reason. The thought of the gun inside the pack made her feel a little safer after last night. Everything that had happened had kept her from sleeping and this morning she was edgy and more than a little nervous. She felt better with Jamison at her side.

She raised an eyebrow at Jamison's pack but didn't comment. "Ready?"

"Lead the way."

"I always do."

Jamison chuckled and she gave her a grin. She wasn't trying to be arrogant and she hoped it didn't come across that way. She liked to make Jamison laugh and her favorite response seemed to do that every time.

She had barely started when she realized the distance between them. She looked over her shoulder. "Are you going to stay way back there?"

"I have a better view from here." Jamison answered and then smiled. "I mean, I can see in all directions."

She shrugged and turned settling into a steady pace. She wished Jamison would run beside her but she had promised to be more understanding and cooperative so she concentrated on her run. Soon the sound of Jamison's footsteps fell into rhythm with her own and she was able to block out all the extra crap from the last couple of weeks. The game on Saturday was going to be huge and she had a lot more hours of footage to watch tonight and tomorrow. Maybe Jamison would join her. She'd been surprised by Jamison's knowledge of football and the Tigers. She hadn't realized Jamison had been watching them all season.

She wondered what Jamison thought about her chances to turn professional. She wondered why Jamison's opinion mattered. If she were honest it was because she cared what Jamison thought. In only a few days, Jamison had become important to her. Last night when she was sitting on Jamison's lap she realized how much more she wanted from her.

"Shea!" Jamison shook her arm. "Did you even see that car back there?"

She looked around and was surprised to find herself on the opposite side of the street. Traffic had increased while she had been daydreaming and she smiled shyly at Jamison. "What car?"

Jamison shook her head. "Go, but please be careful."

She started to jog again but her muscles had already begun to tighten in the few seconds they had been stopped. Her heart wasn't into resuming the run. All she wanted now was to be near Jamison. She slowed her pace and when Jamison didn't appear beside her she slowed even more.

"What are you doing?" Jamison asked softly. Her breath warm in Shea's ear.

"Helping your view."

"Seeing you hasn't been a problem." Silence stretched for a second. "On second thought seeing you has been a problem. A big problem."

She smiled, dropping back beside Jamison and they increased their pace together.

"Why do you do this job?"

"Because I love it," Jamison answered quickly.

"But that could have been a bomb last night."

"Yeah."

"That doesn't worry you?" She glanced at her. "Wait. Have you been in worse situations?"

Jamison smiled. "That's confidential."

"You have been." She knew her voice sounded incredulous but she had never really thought about what Mel or Jamison did at Flagler. "I was scared to death last night and it was just another day on the job for you."

Jamison shrugged.

* * *

Jamison liked to tease Shea but the truth was, words couldn't describe what she had felt last night. She had been scared for Shea's safety and angry at herself for allowing it to happen. Her interest in Shea had clouded her judgment and influenced what demands she placed on Shea. Despite her speech to Shea on Sunday about how things were going to work, her desire to keep Shea happy had influenced her actions.

"Are you good at your job?" Shea asked, interrupting Jamison's thoughts.

She shrugged. "Normally. Not as good as your sister though."

"My sister is perfect at everything." Shea shook her head. Her voice laced with sarcasm, she said, "Still in love with her, huh?"

"There was never anything between me and Mel. She was my training officer and that's it."

"It doesn't matter."

"It does matter." She blocked Shea's path. "It does matter." She stared into Shea's eyes. "It matters to me what you think."

Shea smiled and they both began walking again. When they turned the corner onto Shea's street, her fingertips accidentally brushed Jamison's arm, causing her to shiver involuntarily. Last night she had set the parameters and this morning they were blurred again.

She followed Shea up the steps and into the duplex, securing the door behind them. Her breath caught as Shea's body pushed her hard against the wall. The lines blurred even more as Shea placed her hands on the wall, trapping her in place. Her lips grazing Jamison's ear as she whispered, "When are you going to stop running from me?"

Jamison took a deep breath and closed her eyes. She could feel Shea's warm body pressed against her own. She clenched her fists and fought back against her own desires. "When this case is over," she said with conviction.

She felt Shea's body relax against hers and she opened her eyes.

Shea's face was inches from her own. "Really?"

She couldn't find her voice so she nodded. She was relieved to finally admit her attraction to Shea and she stared longingly at Shea's lips. Soft kissable lips. The memory of their kiss the night before flooded through her and she grasped Shea's waist pulling her closer.

She closed her eyes again bracing for the fire of Shea's kiss but was shocked when she no longer felt the pressure from Shea's body against her own. She opened her eyes in time to see Shea disappear up the stairs. She started to follow her. Shea's voice ricocheted down the stairs.

"Finish the job, Jamison."

Her words hit hard, quickly clearing the haze of desire. *Dammit!* Shea was right. She needed to keep Shea safe or there would be no future with her. She opted for a cold shower instead.

She returned to the kitchen first and was waiting when Shea joined her.

"I need you to go about your day as if I wasn't there. I'm going to follow at a distance and see if I can spot anyone watching you."

Shea frowned. "I like it better when you walk with me." She held up her hand to stop Jamison from responding. "But I understand and will do as you ask."

Jamison smiled and held the door open for her.

"Can we meet back here for lunch?" Shea asked.

"Sure. Do you want me to pick up something?"

"Do we have anything here?" Shea grimaced. "That's edible?"

"Canned tuna?"

"I can live with that."

She followed a good distance behind Shea, focusing her attention on the people around them. Students came in all shapes and sizes and they wore all kinds of clothing. The temperature would reach the high 60s or 70s so most wore shorts. Too long, too short and everything in between. Cargo, athletic and even plaid seemed to be in style. Jamison studied faces and tried to remember if she had noticed any of them before. She remembered Todd's software and wondered if he was making any progress with it or the photo. She hung around outside Shea's classroom until the class was well underway and then stepped outside into the sun. She dialed Todd as she walked toward Carlton's office.

"I'm sorry, Krews. The picture is really dark and grainy. Tech is going to work on it some more but I sent what I had to your email."

"At least it's something. Can you run it through facial recognition?"

"I'm trying. Nothing yet."

"What about your program?"

"It started scanning about seven this morning."

"Thanks, Todd. Get some sleep and call me if anything hits."

"Roger that."

Jamison stepped into the security office and dropped into one of the chairs in front of Carlton's desk. She quickly brought him up to date.

"He probably took the stairs but let's review the camera footage from the elevator anyway."

Carlton nodded and pressed a button on his phone. "Margaret, can you pull the camera footage for level two elevator in the stadium."

"I'll have it for you in five." The phone beeped as she disconnected the line.

Jamison said, "Flagler techs are working on a photo that might be our guy. It's pretty dark because he was outside the light on Shea's porch." She opened her email and studied it for a second before handing it to Carlton.

"Email that to me and I'll show it around to the coaches. Maybe someone will remember him hanging around."

She nodded, sending the email from her phone. She copied Heather on the email too. "Todd called you about the program he wrote, right?"

"Oh yeah. I set him up with a login for our network."

Margaret beeped to advise the footage was in the queue and Carlton was already running through the camera footage on the computer in front of him when Jamison stood up to leave.

"I'll see you at practice," Jamison said and assumed his grunt was an agreement.

A text buzzed her phone as Shea's building came into view. She easily spotted Shea on the steps but slowed to read the text.

Out of class. No u. Heading home.

Right behind u.

Shea came down the stairs and turned toward the duplex. Jamison followed, scanning the crowds around her. Students waved to Shea as she passed but no one's gaze seemed to linger on her. As they approached the house, she picked up her pace and caught up with Shea. Since Shea didn't normally come home at this time of day, she didn't want her to encounter any surprises.

Shea glanced at her in surprise but didn't comment on her sudden appearance. Jamison waited while Shea unlocked the house and then followed her in giving the street one last scan. They dropped their bags on the floor and Jamison began pulling items from the cabinet and refrigerator.

"Wow," she exclaimed as she pulled a jar from the refrigerator. "You have jalapenos."

"I like them on my nachos."

"How is it that you manage to take every healthy item and turn it into trash?" Jamison asked her with a smile.

"Jalapenos are healthy? Yuck. I didn't know."

Shea bumped Jamison's hip as she joined her at the counter.

Jamison dumped diced apple into a bowl and added a scoop of jalapenos. She tore the stems from a handful of spinach and ripped them into small pieces. She added the tuna and some mayonnaise mixing everything in the bowl.

"That almost looks good."

"Don't sound so surprised," Jamison teased her.

"You constantly surprise me," Shea said seriously.

Jamison covered two slices of bread with the tuna mixture and placed the plates on the table.

She turned and smiled at Shea. "That works both ways, you know? I am constantly surprised by you as well."

Shea gave her a devilish smile. "I'm not the cocky asshole you remembered."

"Oh no," Jamison exclaimed. "You're definitely that."

"What?"

Jamison held her hand up and silenced Shea's rebuttal. "But you have some amazing parts too."

Shea dropped into a chair at the table. "You just redeemed yourself."

She set two bottles of water on the table and took the seat across from Shea. This flirty conversation they were having was pulling them closer and Jamison needed to keep some distance between them.

"What does Coach have planned for practice today?"

"I think he wants to tweak several plays so probably quality time with the whiteboard."

"More x's and o's?" Jamison asked.

Shea smiled. "Yep." She took a bite of the sandwich and groaned. "How can this be so good?"

Jamison smiled back at her. "I can work magic."

She watched Shea's eyes darken.

"Don't look at me like that, Shea," she commanded. Placing an elbow on the table and holding her hand in front of Shea, she said, "Hold up your hand."

Shea's eyes still simmered but she did as Jamison asked, placing her elbow on the table too. Jamison put her palm against Shea's and stretched her fingers as far as they would go. Shea's fingers still reached several inches past the tips of Jamison's.

Jamison laughed. "It's no wonder you can throw a football like you do."

"I like to think I have some talent too."

One-handed, Jamison shoved the last bite of her sandwich into her mouth. "I might have noticed that too."

Shea laughed and glanced at the time on her phone. "I need to get to class."

"When you get out of class just head to practice. I'll be behind you."

Shea nodded, placing their plates in the sink and then grabbing her book bag. "I can't wait for this to be over."

CHAPTER ELEVEN

Jamison followed Shea out the door. This new cooperative Shea was starting to grow on her. As usual Shea was dressed in athletic shorts down to her knee and a long-sleeved T-shirt. Jamison watched her greet a few students as she passed and others she gave a wave. At one point, Shea was joined by a large muscular guy and Jamison watched closely, guessing he was a member of the football team. He and Shea parted ways outside her classroom and Jamison took her usual seat in the hallway.

Unable to sit still after a few minutes she got herself coffee from the vending alcove. As usual it tasted horrible and was lukewarm, but she sipped it anyway. At her computer, she stared at the grainy shot of the man outside Shea's house last night. Was this the man who had tried to take out the entire Tallahassee Tigers football team? Everyone assumed he was working alone but did he have the knowledge to cut the brake line on the bus? And where did he get the explosives? So many questions and very few answers.

Ten minutes before Shea's class was to end, Jamison grabbed her bag and walked out into the sun. She took a seat on a concrete decorative wall outside the building. When Shea passed her Jamison scrutinized the area and the students around her. She didn't see anyone with a camera or even anyone whose focus was solely on Shea. They would give her a wave but then return their attention to their group. Most lone individuals were either on their way to or from class or scanning their phone. She was constantly impressed with their ability to walk and type with their faces and fingers glued to the device they carried.

Shea went straight to her locker and began dressing for practice as Jamison quickly searched and cleared the locker room. As she pulled open the supply closet, pointing her pistol inside, she thought about the day Shea was locked inside. Now that she knew Shea's routine, she wondered why Lynnette hadn't missed Shea before the game.

"Shea, why didn't Lynnette notice you weren't waiting to get taped the day you were locked in the closet?"

Shea looked up from tying her cleats. "She tapes me several hours before the game starts. We'd already run some drills on the field and I'd returned here to relax for a while."

"Is that your normal routine?"

"Yeah. I like to come back here for a little quiet time before we take the field for the game. The guys are rowdy and play their music loud."

Jamison nodded.

Shea threaded her fingers through the face guard on her helmet, gathering it and her shoulder pads together. "I can see your wheels turning. Want to share?"

"I'm just thinking."

Jamison waited by the coaches' office until Coach Sutton was finished going over x's and o's on the whiteboard and then she followed Shea to the field. Today she didn't head straight for Carlton but scanned the sidelines for Lynnette. Jamison waited until she was alone and then approached her.

"Lynnette, did anything strange happen the day Shea was locked in the supply closet?"

Lynnette, wearing shorts and a T-shirt with the team logo, watched the players as she thought for a minute. "It was a crazy day. Game days normally are, though. I hated that I wasn't in the locker room because I would have noticed Shea wasn't there. Honestly, I don't know how everyone didn't notice she wasn't there."

"If you weren't in the locker room, where were you?"

She motioned to the equipment bag in front of her. "We pack these on Friday for use during the game but that day they weren't properly packed. I had to run back and forth between the main supply room downstairs and the field to get them prepared."

"Did you pack them on Friday like normal?"

Lynnette studied her. "We did but I just assumed one of the guys had pulled things from it after practice instead of using the supplies from the locker room." She shrugged. "It's not normally what happens but like I said, things are crazy on game day."

Jamison nodded, watching the team run through drills on the field.

"You're the first person that's asked me about that day."

"The police didn't question everyone?" Jamison asked, glancing at her.

"They did a group questioning and asked if we saw anything. I didn't because I was so busy."

Jamison looked at the field again. Being on the sideline gave a different perspective than sitting in the stands. Not so broad a view but she felt more like part of the action. "Do you think someone not a part of the team could have accessed the bags and moved the supplies?"

"No."

"Okay. Thanks." Jamison started to walk away.

"Hey." Lynnette stepped close to her again. "Do you think someone on the team is responsible for all of this?"

"Not necessarily. Like you said, one of the other athletic trainers might have removed the supplies and it was only a coincidence."

"But you don't believe in coincidences?"

"Oh I believe in them." Jamison shrugged. "I just don't like them."

* * *

Jamison climbed the stairs to where Carlton sat and slid into the chair beside him. "Does the same security officer watch the hallway for each home game?"

Carton looked at her. "No. Crowd control is the worst job so I don't want anyone stuck with it at every game."

She nodded. "Do you have a schedule of where everyone worked each game?"

"Where are you going with this?" Carlton asked her defensively.

She shrugged. "Just an avenue to explore." She wasn't trying to piss Carlton off. She needed his cooperation. "Can you say positively that the officer assigned to the hallway was involved in settling the disruption in the student section that day?"

Carlton thought for a moment and then nodded. "Jeremy was questioned extensively by me and TPD. He didn't see anyone hanging around except reporters and he was on the arrest paperwork for two of the students that TPD ended up hauling away."

"Did he recognize the reporters? Or identify them from their badges?"

Carlton frowned and picked up his radio. "He's on duty now. Let's ask him." He keyed the radio. "Officer Warrick?"

A youthful voice responded immediately. "Yeah, Chief?"

"Can you join me in the stadium?"

"Yes sir." An engine started. "About ten minutes out."

Carlton sat back in his seat. "My guys took a lot of heat when the notes started appearing. With the campus closed on Sundays and the stadium locked, TPD didn't want to look any further for a suspect." He sighed. "I vetted each one of them myself before they were hired. Backgrounds and interviews with anyone that knew them. They're a good bunch of guys and girls. I trust them all."

"That's good to know." She paused, letting the silence stretch between them. "I didn't mean to imply I was accusing anyone. Having a different officer dealing with the press at each game means someone could sneak into their ranks and not be noticed."

"Okay." He thought for a second. "We have a campus paper and their reporter should be in that pack every week."

She tilted her head. "Can you track that avenue and see if it's the same reporter every week?"

"I can. I know it's the same byline each week. Crystal Bailey. Home and Away." He nodded toward the tunnel entrance. "There's Jeremy."

"I'll let you do the talking, Chief." He smiled and she was glad the tension between them had eased.

Jeremy entered the row beneath them and remained standing. "Yes, Chief?"

Jamison glanced at him. His youthful voice had been deceiving. Up close she could see he was a little older than she first thought. She watched the play on the field and quickly located Shea in the huddle. As usual she could hear Shea's strong voice call the cadence before faking a handoff and throwing a pass twenty yards down the field. Carlton's voice brought her back to the conversation beside her.

"Jeremy, are you familiar with the members of the press that hang around outside the locker rooms?"

He grimaced. "Not really, Chief. I know one or two of the local guys because they visit during the week for other events too. Oh and the ESPN ones, 'cause I see them on the TV."

"So when you told TPD there were only reporters in the hallway the day of the incident with Shea Carter what did you base that on?"

"Oh, I checked their badges. Right before the call came in for the fight I went down the line and checked them all." He glanced at Jamison. "No one is allowed in that area except press," he explained.

"Okay, Jeremy. Good job," Carlton said, dismissing him with a nod.

Jeremy turned to go but Carlton called out to him. "Was Crystal Bailey in that hallway too?"

Jeremy looked back. "Yeah, she was there."

"Can you track her down and bring her back here?"

Jeremy nodded. "Sure, Chief. I'll get right on it."

Jamison watched Jeremy walk away. "He seems like a good kid."

"I hired him right out of high school. His mother works on campus in the billing department and in the summers he would come with her. The kid would follow me everywhere." Carlton laughed. "He knew the job better than some of my officers. He even made copies of the manuals and took them home to study."

She laughed with him. "How could you not hire someone with that kind of dedication?"

"That's what I thought too. He's my only employee without a college degree so I've got him working on one." Carlton shifted in his seat, getting more comfortable. "How's our cub doing?"

Jamison groaned. "She's become more cooperative as the week's progressed."

"That's good to hear," he said with a hint of pride in his voice. "I knew she'd come around."

Jamison glanced at him. Shea was one of his kids and he looked like a father whose daughter had taken her first steps.

They chatted about the upcoming game against Jacksonville while they watched the Tigers finish their practice and head for the locker room. Shea waited at the tunnel entrance until Jamison caught up with her. In the weight room, Shea dropped her shoulder pads and helmet at Jamison's feet and began her lifting cycle.

She watched Shea push the bar high over her head without a pause and she realized Shea's ribs were no longer bothering her. Either the pain was gone or Shea was ignoring it. She had admired Shea's outer beauty for a while but what she hadn't seen on first glance stood out to her now. Shea's strength and endurance. Her stubborn dedication. Shea didn't quit no matter what. For the first time, Jamison realized that no one on the team had given a thought to not playing a game. Either in the beginning when the notes first started coming and not even now when things had gotten crazy. In her talks with Shea, they had never discussed quitting as an option because it wasn't.

* * *

Shea glanced up from the weights to locate Jamison as she had started doing between each set, casually hoping no one noticed. Just looking at Jamison leaning against the wall brought her comfort. And made her smile.

The outer locker room door opened and Chief Hammer walked in. He motioned for Jamison to follow him. Had something happened? When Jamison reached the door she glanced back her eyes finding Shea's. Jamison's smile reassured her that everything was okay.

She returned to her sets but her mind was on Jamison. The weights she'd lost track of slammed against each other making a loud smack. The guys around her laughed and the harassment went on for a few minutes until everyone returned to their sets. She tried to clear her mind but every time she began to relax into her workout thoughts of Jamison pulled her back.

* * *

"Want me to place an officer in the weight room to keep an eye on the cub?" Carlton asked Jamison softly.

She shook her head. "She won't leave except through this door."

Carlton tilted his head. "You really did come to a truce, didn't you?" He nodded as if that was the outcome he had always expected. Turning to a young girl in jeans and a peace T-shirt waiting in the hallway with Jeremy, he said, "Crystal, this is Jamison. She'd like to ask you a few questions about your fellow members of the press and the day Shea Carter was locked in the supply closet."

Jamison leaned casually against the wall as she studied the girl. She looked more curious than scared and seemed to be studying Jamison too. "You cover all the home and away games, right?"

Crystal nodded.

"So you're familiar with all the reporters that crowd the hallway before and after the games?"

"There's usually one or two I don't know from the opposing team especially if it's not a team we play every year. I've been the Tiger reporter for two years now," she said with pride.

"Do you remember anything about the reporters you didn't recognize on that Saturday?"

Crystal wrinkled her face in concentration. "That was the North Carolina game so I knew everyone." She paused. "When Jeremy left we thought Shea was already in the other locker room so we all moved to the tunnel entrance to see the team take the field. She's the only reason we watch that hallway."

Jamison shrugged at Carlton. "That answers my questions. At least we know he didn't have a press pass."

The locker room door beside Jamison opened and Shea stepped out, gave everyone a nod and then continued toward her locker room.

"Thanks, Carlton." Jamison followed Shea.

Holding her pistol close to her body she stepped in closing the door behind them. She quickly secured the area and returned to wait for Shea by the door. While Shea took her ice bath and then showered, Jamison thought about the other ways someone could get into the secure area during a game. During the week a student ID would get them past the badge readers but not on a game day. There were no vendors in that area so a team badge would have to be the only way. She pulled open the locker room door and was pleased to see Carlton and Jeremy still standing in the hallway.

"Carlton," Jamison called to him.

He motioned for Jeremy to stay where he was and walked down the hallway to Jamison. "Everything okay?"

"Did you pull a list of the badge swipes into the team area that day?"

"I did and there were no unauthorized entries. I don't think anyone would hold the door for someone they didn't recognize."

She nodded. "Has anyone lost their badge since the season started?"

"That's a pretty big deal around here and only my staff or I can replace it for them. We document any replacements." He thought for a minute before continuing. "Now the registrar's office makes their first badge, so they do have the equipment to make them." He frowned. "But they're not supposed to. I'll make a trip over there first thing in the morning when they open. It's all full-time staff and they don't allow any students to work in there."

"If someone did a favor at least we'll know whose badge we're looking for and maybe we can catch a camera angle."

Shea stepped out of the locker room and smiled at Carlton.

He grinned back and gave her a little hug. "Ready for Saturday?"

"Of course," Shea said confidently.

"Thanks for everything, Carlton," Jamison said as she and Shea turned to leave.

CHAPTER TWELVE

"Are you going to tell me what all that was about?" Shea asked.

"Just following every avenue someone could use to access your area. You didn't hear any of the team talking about losing their badge did you?"

Shea shook her head. "That's a big deal. Usually the guys just piggyback with someone else until the season is over rather than report it to security."

"Well that's stupid," Jamison said without thinking. She saw Shea glance at her and then smiled. "Sorry. First thought slipped out."

"No, you're right. It is stupid. They don't think about who might be using their badge, only that they're going to get in trouble if they report it."

Jamison scanned the open commons area as they exited the stadium. As usual the few students around were hurrying to or from class. No one seemed to be lingering this late in the evening. Probably other areas of campus had students hanging out but around the stadium it was mostly empty. She could hear shouts of an intramural game in progress on the practice field but they turned in the opposite direction.

They walked in silence for a few minutes. "What's on the menu tonight, Chef Krews?" Shea asked teasingly.

She frowned. "I'm not sure. There's more chicken left. We could try last night's dinner again."

"Nothing exotic and disgustingly healthy?"

"If exotic is what you are looking for? Let's see..." She contemplated the ingredients she had purchased. "I think there might be some bean sprouts and rice noodles. We could do a Pad Thai mix. Do you have any fish sauce?"

"Seriously. How can you even ask me if I have something so disgusting?"

"You don't even know what it is?"

Shea laughed. "Okay. I don't but I do know it sounds disgusting."

"Well, you wanted exotic."

Shea glanced at her. "Have you been all over the world?"

"I've been to a few places."

"Where was the weirdest?"

Jamison was silent for a few moments. "That would probably be my first mission with your sister."

"There's my damn sister again," Shea growled.

Jamison bumped her hip. "Do you want to hear about this place or not?"

"Tell your story just keep the mention of my sister to a minimum."

Jamison laughed. "I'd only been an agent for a couple months but Flagler needed a package picked up at a secluded retreat outside Beijing. They wanted Mel because she'd been there before and knew their customs. She grilled me on background for the two days it took to coordinate and then get there. We were supposed to fly in, pick up the package and fly out. Easy, right?"

"Right."

"Everything went smooth until we arrived at the retreat." Jamison scanned the street. It was deserted except for a few parked empty vehicles including her own. "We were greeted at the door, which I now know is not the usual custom, by a man dressed in this white scrubs-looking outfit. He opened the door and bowed to us. Mel responded in kind but the problem was she hadn't removed her shoes yet because we weren't even inside. Apparently if you don't follow all rituals you are refused access and the first ritual is you must remove your shoes before greeting anyone already inside the retreat."

"So she was supposed to snub him until her shoes were removed?"

"I guess. We had to call in and explain why we now had to stay the night. Mel was furious." Jamison recalled the late night surveillance trip back to the retreat and their subsequent pursuit of the man. "We returned the next day to pick up the package."

Shea frowned as she stepped onto her porch, triggering the motion detector lights. She crossed to the door and inserted her key. "What aren't you telling me?"

Jamison smiled. "The man was trying to steal whatever was in the package so he had set us up to give himself an extra day to scan the retreat."

"Really? That's so cloak-and-dagger. What was in the package?"

Jamison shrugged reaching around her to open the door.

"You don't know?" Shea asked indignantly as she stepped into the house.

"It's not my job to know what's in the package but only to pick up and deliver." Jamison flipped on the kitchen lights and her gaze caught on a bouquet of red roses sitting on the kitchen table. She immediately pulled her pistol and stepped in front of Shea.

"I can't believe you don't look—"

Jamison began slowly moving backward pushing Shea out the door as she kept her pistol pointed in front of her. With her free hand, she pulled her truck keys from her pocket and passed them to Shea. "Wait in my truck."

"But I want—"

"Please, Shea. Now," she said with urgency.

Shea didn't hesitate.

Jamison waited until Shea was inside the truck and then she slowly entered the house again. She pulled a flashlight from her bag and held it away from her body to avoid silhouetting herself. She moved through each room checking every possible hiding place and then climbed the stairs. Shea's room seemed untouched and once she confirmed there was no one hiding in the closet or bathroom she returned to the kitchen. Securing the door behind her, she pulled out her phone.

"It's Jamison Krews. I need to talk with Todd or whoever is in charge tonight."

"I can get Todd for you, Agent Krews," a male voice responded immediately. "Hang on."

"Jamison?" Bowden's tense voice came on the line. "What's wrong?"

"Someone's broken into Ms. Carter's house." Jamison tried to keep the waver out of her voice. "I'm taking her to my residence and I need an agent to meet me there."

"I'm dispatching Liam now. Are you secure?"

"Yes, I've cleared the house and we're in my truck." Jamison climbed in beside Shea. "Can you have someone pull the tape for today?"

"Yes, and I'll monitor the live feed until you return."

"Thank you." Jamison hit redial on Heather's last call.

Heather picked up immediately.

"Heather. We had a break-in. Can you meet me at Shea's in about twenty minutes? I'm taking her somewhere secure."

"I'm on my way."

Jamison tossed the phone into the middle console. She glanced at Shea. Her face was tense, her body pulled up tight under a coat of Jamison's she had found behind the seat. She gently placed her hand on Shea's thigh. "Are you okay?"

"Fine." She shrugged. "Just feeling a little vulnerable at the moment."

"I'm taking you somewhere safe."

Shea gave her a little smile. "Thank you."

Jamison pulled to a stop in front of the glass and metal futuristic-looking building that housed her apartment, parking directly in front of the entrance.

At the elevator, she scanned her badge and they rose to the fourth floor. She scanned her badge again to exit the elevator foyer and then unlocked her door. Shea watched her closely and Jamison could see her curiosity.

"Where are we?" Shea asked softly. "Is this one of your company's safe houses?"

The elevator door dinged open behind them and Jamison's hand immediately went to her pistol. Liam Russo swiped his badge to exit the foyer and approached her open front door. She gave him a relieved smile. "Thanks for coming."

"You saved me from a boring debrief." He stepped inside, closed the door and he held out his hand to Shea. "Liam."

"Shea." She glanced at Jamison. "Are you leaving me here?"

She didn't say "with him" but Jamison knew what she was asking.

"Excuse us for a second," Jamison said to Liam. Taking Shea's hand, she led her into the bedroom. "I have to go back to your place and do a more thorough search."

"Can't Heather do that?"

Jamison sighed. She was anxious to check out the house and see what the cameras caught. "She could but I want to be there too."

Shea looked around the room and Jamison could see her taking in the small single bed and the dresser with one picture. Shea crossed and picked up the picture. Looking closely, she quickly glanced up at Jamison. "That's you," she said in surprise, looking around the room again. "This is your place?"

"It is." She shrugged. "I'm not here much."

Shea sat down on the bed and ran her hand over the comforter. "How long will you be gone?"

Jamison crossed and knelt in front of her. "I'll be back as soon as I can."

She pressed her lips gently to Shea's and then stood.

"Liam's a really good guy but you can stay in here if you want." She opened the cabinet to display a television. "Make yourself at home. There's sweats and more comfortable clothes in the dresser." She stopped at the door and gave Shea a reassuring smile. "You'll be safe here."

She found Liam in the kitchen combing through her cabinets. She pulled open a drawer and removed a stack of carryout menus. "Get her a pizza with everything from Pizza Zone." She motioned toward the closed bedroom door. "Food will draw her out. She's a little shook up right now."

"We'll be fine, Krews. Take off."

"Thanks again. Call if you need anything."

* * *

Shea slowly opened the bedroom door as soon as she heard the front door slam. She was starving and ordering pizza was her first priority. As she approached the kitchen she heard Liam ordering two large pizzas with everything. She rested one hip against the small kitchen table and waited until he disconnected the call.

"Thanks for ordering pizza."

He gave her a wink. "Jamison suggested it."

She should have known Jamison would take care of everything. Turning, she scanned the room. A small kitchen opened into a larger living room. A dark brown leather couch took up one wall and a large bookcase filled with DVDs took up another. Shea ran her hand across the back of the couch as she walked toward the bookcase.

"Want to watch a movie?" She wished she had her film footage but instead she would relax tonight and worry about getting caught up tomorrow.

"Sounds like a good plan." He set two bottles of water on the coffee table.

Shea chose an action adventure movie and slid it into the player. She took the opposite end of the couch from Liam and pulled a jumbo-sized leather footstool between them. "Shall we get comfortable?"

Liam placed his knee across the footstool and rested his other leg on top of it. Shea pulled a blanket from the back of the couch, curling under it. She wished she had told Jamison to be careful.

CHAPTER THIRTEEN

Jamison's truck slid to a stop in front of Shea's duplex. Heather crossed the street to join her on the porch. Jamison's phone vibrated and she smiled at the text message from Shea. *Be careful.* She dialed Flagler and was passed to Bowden immediately.

"Techs are scanning today's footage. Nothing yet. No one has been near the house since you left. How is Ms. Carter?"

"She's fine. Thanks for sending Liam and watching the house. TPD is with me and we're going in now." She paused. "Could you send the bomb dog? After last night, I don't want to trust us to see everything."

"They're already on their way. Keep in touch."

Jamison gave Heather a smile. "Let's clear the place again. My first check was pretty quick. A bomb dog is on its way."

"I'll let you lead the way," Heather said.

Jamison unlocked the door and they both stepped inside with weapons drawn. Slowly they walked through each room until they were confident the house was empty. Jamison returned to the kitchen first to take a closer look at the flowers.

Propped against the vase was another Polaroid picture. Shea sitting on Jamison's lap with their lips frozen inches apart. It was taken through Shea's living room window. Jamison cursed as she stuffed it into a plastic bag and then into her pocket. She looked up to find Heather watching her.

Jamison sighed and handed her the picture. "It's not what it looks like?"

Heather raised her eyebrows.

"Oh hell. It is what it looks like but that's the extent of what happened. It was taken yesterday before I noticed the package of explosives."

"That explains why he was still lurking when you guys stepped outside," Heather volunteered.

Jamison picked up her laptop. "Let's wait outside until the bomb team finishes."

She dropped the tailgate on her truck and rested her open laptop on it. She logged into the cameras and began scanning the previous night. She could guess pretty close to the exact time this picture was taken and it didn't take her long to find him on camera. Since he was out of the view of the motion detector porch lights, the camera was working in night vision. A hood covered his head but they could see he wasn't very tall. They watched him gently place a square object on the ground in front of the window and step onto it.

"What does he have?" Heather asked, leaning in for a better view.

"Recycling bin, I think."

"He looks about five foot seven or eight," Heather guessed.

"Yeah." Jamison looked up as a dark SUV approached. She placed a reassuring hand on her pistol.

A short dark-haired woman emerged followed by a large dog. "I'm with Flagler," she called as she approached them. She carried a bag in one hand and held the leash in her other.

"Jamison Krews." She nodded at Heather. "TPD Officer Heather Cannon."

"I'm Kinsey." She lifted the slack in the leash and nodded at the dog sitting at her feet. "This is Jack and he'll be sniffing your house this evening." She smiled at both of them. "Jack prefers to work alone. Can you both wait out here, please?"

Holding her laptop against her chest, Jamison watched the quiet street.

"So, you want to talk about that picture?" Heather asked with a smile.

Jamison grimaced but before she could answer her cell phone buzzed. "Saved by the bell."

"Jamison, we have something. I'll let Todd give you the details," Bowden explained.

Jamison motioned for Heather to follow and they climbed into her truck.

"Krews?" Todd spoke quickly. "Are you there? This is really good."

"Go ahead, Todd. You're on speaker. Officer Cannon with TPD is with me."

"Okay. Greetings, Officer Cannon. On to the good stuff. We caught him delivering the roses about four this afternoon. He either didn't know the camera was there or he didn't care. We have a full facial shot, which I sent to your email. He's not a student at TU so I'm running him through the DMV. Also, my facial recognition software running the area around the stadium found multiple matches to him."

Jamison already had her laptop open and was logging into her email. "I got the picture, Todd." She angled the screen so Heather could see too.

"Holy shit. I know that guy," Heather exclaimed. "I interviewed him yesterday. His mother owns a white Honda Accord and we went to her house. He answered the door." She pulled her notebook from her pocket and flipped through a couple pages. "George Henry McGomery, the second. He said he didn't drive and DMV confirmed no license. There was a bicycle on the porch. He claimed he didn't live there but got evasive when we asked for his address. When we interviewed his mother she said he did live there but was shy and didn't like to tell people he lived with his mother."

"Are you getting this, Todd?"

"Yep. I'm already searching other databases. Currently he works for Watson-Hughes. It's a small data entry company on Thomasville Road."

"Send me everything, Todd. As soon as the dog sniffer is finished we'll start with his mother and see if we can locate him." Jamison glanced at Heather. She didn't ask if it was okay and Heather didn't seem eager to call in TPD backup.

Heather nodded. "Let's get this guy."

Kinsey and Jack stepped onto the porch. "All clear," she said as Jamison approached. "He stuttered in the living room but then couldn't locate anything specifically. My boss says you had a device in there last night."

Jamison nodded. "Sam turned it over to the FBI."

"Yeah, he said not to worry about the stutter. It was probably leftover scents. The rest of the house was clear."

"Thanks for coming so quickly."

"Anytime." She gave Heather a nod and crossed the street to her SUV.

Jamison climbed the steps and secured the front door. "Let's go get him."

Heather nodded. "We'll take my car." Seeing Jamison's hesitation she continued. "I have lights and a siren, a radio for backup and a backseat to put him in."

Jamison shrugged her surrender.

"And a badge to arrest him," Heather continued.

"Okay. Okay." Jamison moved to the passenger side of the blue sedan and climbed in. She sat silently and listened as TPD units radioed dispatch from all over the city. She recognized a few codes that were universal. The voices were monotone and she assumed it was only normal activity.

Heather picked up the radio as soon as she turned onto Krest Street. "Dispatch. Seven zero four."

"Go ahead seven zero four," a female voice responded immediately.

"Myself and Flagler Agent Krews will be ten seventeen at two twenty-three Krest Street."

"Ten four, seven zero four. Twenty fifteen hours."

Heather dropped the volume several clicks. "Just letting dispatch know we'll be conducting an investigation. I think we should give a knock on the door and see if Mom will help us bring her boy in easy." She shrugged. "But if you want to go in hard I can call for backup."

"No, easy is good with me."

Within minutes, they arrived at the McGomery residence and parked in front of the house. They casually approached the front door. The house was a peach color with a large picture window. There were lights on upstairs and downstairs. Heather tapped lightly on the glass in the door, bypassing the doorbell. A woman's face appeared in the window. Heather held up her badge and identification. "TPD, ma'am. We need to speak with you."

The woman who slowly opened the door wore nurse scrubs and clearly had not been home long. Her hair was tied in a ponytail and loose strands dangled in front of her face.

"Can we come in, Mrs. McGomery?" Heather stepped into the open doorway giving her little option to say no.

Jamison followed as they entered a small living room. An aroma of garlic drifted in from the kitchen.

"We spoke yesterday concerning your vehicle." Heather waited until the woman nodded. "We need to speak with your son again. Is he home?"

"Yes. He's upstairs in his room."

Jamison stepped forward. "Ma'am, can you call him down, please?"

The woman went to the foot of the staircase. "George, can you come down here."

They heard movement upstairs and Heather moved in front of Jamison motioning for Mrs. McGomery to take a step back.

"Is dinner ready?" George called as he came into view, his footsteps heavy on the stairs. His gaze quickly took in the women.

Heather said, "We spoke yesterday, George. Do you remember?"

He nodded.

"We have a few more questions for you but we need to ask them at the station. Can you come with us?"

He nodded again and as he drew even with Heather he sprinted for the front door.

Jamison used his forward momentum and gave him a hard shove into the front door. He bounced back and she grabbed his arm swinging him around as she swept his legs out from under him. They tumbled to the floor with Jamison on top. She pulled his arm behind his back and Heather slapped a cuff on his other wrist, then secured both wrists and pulled him to his feet. His mother seemed frozen in place.

"Why'd you do that, George?" Heather asked him.

He shrugged.

"Let's go." Heather pushed him toward the front door, walked him across the lawn and put him in the back of the car. She could hear Heather reciting his Miranda rights before she shut the door.

"What about her?" Jamison nodded to George's mother who stood on the porch watching.

Heather approached Mrs. McGomery. "He's going to be detained for a while. As soon as we get things worked out he can call you."

"Is he...is he under arrest?"

"Yes, ma'am. There's no need for you to come to the station until he calls you. Okay?" Heather explained again.

She nodded and stepped back inside the house.

Heather walked back to where Jamison stood by the car. "Do you want to come with me or I can I call you a car?"

"I'd like to go with you."

Heather picked up the radio microphone as soon as the car was moving. "Seven zero four, Dispatch."

"Go ahead seven zero four." This time a male voice acknowledged Heather's call.

"Myself and Flagler Agent Krews are ten seventeen, ten seventy-two back to the station."

"Ten four. Twenty forty-eight hours."

Heather glanced at Jamison. "Prisoner in custody," she explained.

"I thought it was something like that." Jamison was silent for a few moments. "Did this all seem a little too easy to you?"

"What? Seeing his face on camera and then scooping him up?"

Jamison smiled and glanced in the back at George. With his hands cuffed behind him, he was shifted sideways on the seat and had his knees pulled up to his chest. He stared out the side window, his dark straggly hair hanging over his eyes. "George, who put you up to this?"

Heather glanced at her and then back at the road.

She gave a shrug when he didn't answer. She wasn't sure of her role with Heather but she knew she wanted answers from this guy. When Heather didn't stop her, she continued.

"George." Jamison waited until he looked at her. His eyes grew large as he saw Jamison's face for the first time and clearly recognized her.

"Rot in hell," he mumbled under his breath.

Jamison glanced at Heather and she nodded for her to continue. "Who's going to rot in hell, George?"

"You." He stared out the window again.

"Why am I going to rot in hell, George?"

"Because of her. It's all her fault. Everything is her fault."

"George. George, look at me." Jamison pushed him harder. "Why is it her fault?"

He glanced at her and then back out the window. "I'm not saying anything else."

Jamison turned in her seat and spoke softly to Heather. "What do you think?"

"I think you're correct. It was all too easy but sometimes you don't get past easy and easy closes the case."

Jamison grimaced. "So we're done."

"Oh no." Heather shook her head. "Have Todd send me everything he's compiled. I think that'll be enough to get a search warrant for his house."

"Okay."

Jamison unbuckled her seat belt as they pulled to a stop in front of the TPD station. She had never been inside and she stared in through the glass windows at the flurry of activity. It was a hulking building made of white stone and Jamison could see why people found it intimidating.

Heather radioed dispatch that they had arrived and then pulled George from the backseat. Jamison followed them inside. They maneuvered down several halls until they reached an interview room. Heather deposited George at the table facing the mirror. Closing the door, she led Jamison to the next room. She hit a few buttons on the console and then took a seat at the computer. "We're taping now and you'll be able to hear everything that's said. Call Todd. Let's get the search warrant started. It might take a while."

Jamison dialed Todd and asked him to email all specifics in locating George McGomery. She also gave him an update on the arrest for Bowden.

Using her cell phone Heather dialed FBI Special Agent Wallace and advised him of the arrest. Then picked up the phone on the console beside her. "Tanner. I need an officer outside interrogation two. And I need someone to walk a search warrant to the judge on call." She paused while the officer on the other end responded to her demands. "I'll be done in five. Thanks." She slammed the phone back on the console and began typing.

Jamison opened the email on her phone. "I have all of Todd's information. I'm forwarding it to you now."

Heather nodded but continued typing. She hit print on her screen and switched to email, printing Todd's information to attach to the search warrant. "Give me a chance to get some information from him and if that doesn't work you can come in and rile him up again." She smiled at Jamison. "He seems to really like you."

"I have that effect on deranged lunatics."

Heather carried her printed paperwork outside the room but when she appeared on the other side of the glass her hands were empty. She sat down across from George and stared at him for a few minutes. "Are you ready to talk now, George?"

He stared down at the table.

"George, did you put the roses in Shea Carter's house?" Heather asked.

"I might have."

"Why did you do it?"

"So she would know I can get to her."

"Why do you want to get to her?"

Jamison watched his face as his eyes began to light with excitement.

"She can't play on Saturday. The Tigers are a horrible team and don't deserve to be in the championship. We asked them nicely not to play but they wouldn't listen."

Heather jumped on his first mention of others being involved. "Who asked them not to play, George?"

He looked down at the table again as he realized his mistake and then back at her. "I asked them not to play," he said with renewed vigor.

"Okay." Heather nodded. "Why did you ask them not to play?"

"I told you. The Tigers are horrible and they don't deserve to be in the playoffs."

Heather paused and Jamison could see her processing his statement before she spoke again.

"Okay, George. The Tigers are horrible. Who are we going to cheer for?"

"Atlanta, of course." He sighed as if she had finally asked the important question.

Heather nodded. "Of course, Atlanta."

She turned and looked at Jamison through the window. At a knock on the door Heather stood and left the room.

Jamison left the viewing room and joined Heather in the hallway. Special Agent Wallace gave Jamison a nod but spoke to Heather.

"I want to talk with him."

Heather nodded and looked at an approaching uniformed officer. He handed her a piece of paper and she glanced at it before making eye contact with Wallace. "Search warrant. Do you want to go with us or stay here and question him?"

He seemed torn for a moment but quickly made a decision. "I'll stay here and question him but I'll send bomb techs with you."

Heather glanced at Jamison and then nodded. "I'll text you the address to send them to. Let's go."

CHAPTER FOURTEEN

"The transfer of information has been very one sided so far," Heather said as she picked up the radio microphone and advised dispatch they were headed back to the previous address to execute a search warrant.

Jamison didn't answer Heather's comment. Jamison worked more with the CIA than the FBI but she knew large organizations tended to hold their information close. She was glad she worked with Flagler. They didn't have law enforcement privileges but over the years they had developed positive relationships with the agencies they worked with and normally that meant an even flow of information.

Heather sent a text and then dropped the car into gear. "Mom's about to get a big surprise."

"I think you arrested him so fast she didn't have time to think about it," Jamison said, glancing at a new text alert.

"Yeah, I thought we'd get some resistance from her."

"Flagler has an update. Want to hear it now?"

"Yeah, sure."

Jamison dialed Flagler and placed Todd on speaker. "Heather is with me and you're on speaker, Todd."

"Greetings again, Officer Cannon," Todd said in a computer voice before switching back to a more serious tone. "I found some interesting background on McGomery's employer, Watson-Hughes. The first founding owner was widower Shelley Watson and she passed away several years ago. She has two sons who aren't active in the company. In fact, both live in California. The second founding owner is Charles Hughes. He's had a long career in doing absolutely nothing. After leaving the military in nineteen seventy-two he bounced around until teaming up with Shelley Watson about ten years ago. The company has a fairly reputable name although Mr. Hughes' name has been linked to Clayton Thomas on multiple occasions."

"The head of the Mountain Militia?" Heather asked, pulling to a stop in front of the McGomery house.

"That's the guy."

"Where's the connection, Todd?" Jamison asked.

"I'm still working on that. I'll get back with you."

Heather looked at Jamison. "Are you familiar with Clayton Thomas?"

Jamison shook her head. "Not a bit."

"Understandable. He's worked hard to stay under the radar. I ran into a few guys from his group a couple years ago. They were in town blowing off some steam because apparently they don't get away from the compound much. They got in a fight with some college boys and it turned into a major brawl. The bouncers kicked them all out but they continued fighting in the parking lot. When we finally got them separated, we grilled them all for a few hours before Clayton Thomas showed up and bailed them out."

"What was the fight about?"

"We were never really sure. The college boys said they were hitting on one of the guys' girlfriends but the Militia boys wouldn't say much." Heather opened a search engine on the computer mounted between the seats. "There isn't much available information about the Mountain Militia, just their website. But basically once you're a member, you're in for life." She swiveled the computer so Jamison could see the Mountain Militia homepage.

"Looks like the typical white supremacists against the government organization."

Heather nodded. "With an added bonus of being law abiding. We've heard talk that they're stockpiling guns and ammunition but the Feds haven't been able to find a reason to get inside." She shrugged. "I don't know how hard they've tried. Too many other active groups they have to watch on a regular basis. I do know the FBI has a file on them because I did some checking after the fight." She opened her car door. "Let's go make Momma's night."

Jamison glanced at the dark house and then at her watch. "It's not even ten but I think Momma might be in bed," she said softly as they approached.

Heather nodded and rapped on the glass window in the door. After a couple of attempts, she pressed the doorbell. Within seconds, Mrs. McGomery's face appeared in the glass.

Heather held up her badge and identification. "Ma'am, it's Officer Cannon again. Can you open the door?"

Mrs. McGomery slowly pulled open the door. "I was in bed. I took a sleeping pill because well…you know." She shrugged and stared at the floor.

Jamison took a step back as the smell of alcohol emanating from the woman overwhelmed her. She glanced at Heather who had her eyes focused on Mrs. McGomery.

Heather placed her hand on the open door and stepped inside. "We have a warrant to search George's room and any common areas. Why don't you have a seat right there, Mrs. McGomery?" Heather guided her to the sofa and steadied her while she took a seat. "Which room is George's?"

"To the left. The spare bedroom is to the right," Mrs. McGomery answered.

"Has George ever had any friends stay the night?" Heather asked.

"No. No, George doesn't really have any friends."

Heather nodded and turned to Jamison. "Just the one on the left then. I'll send the other crew up when they arrive. I'll look around down here."

Jamison nodded and climbed the stairs. George's bedroom door was shut and locked. She pulled out her set of picks and quickly opened it. Sliding on gloves she walked once around the room, glancing at anything in the open. The room was neat and orderly. A laptop sat open on the desk and she touched the keyboard to wake it up. George had been in the middle of writing an email to screen name MM103. She quickly scanned the email and then pulled out her phone and snapped a shot of the email.

There were no pictures or posters anywhere. A bookshelf held high school textbooks and a few mystery novels. Under the laptop was a ticket to an Atlanta Wildcats football game dated two weeks prior. She snapped a picture of it too. In his closet two bins held his socks and underwear. T-shirts and dress shirts were hung along with dress pants and jeans. Several pairs of shoes were lined up beneath the clothes. She turned at the sound of footsteps on the stairs. A dark-haired woman entered the room followed by two men. The second man, dressed in jeans and running shoes, held the leash on a large short-haired brown dog. The other two wore black suits identifying themselves as FBI agents.

The woman approached Jamison. "Agent Krews? I'm Sheldon Barrett. That's Terry Haus and Willie Armentrout on the leash."

Jamison nodded and shook each of their hands. "It's pretty sparse in here," she said, stepping out of the room. The two agents in suits joined her, leaving Willie and his dog to work.

Barrett's eyes were on Willie as he maneuvered around the room while she spoke to Jamison. "Nothing of interest?"

Jamison relayed the few items inside the room that she had found. "My guess is he spends most of his spare time on the computer."

Barrett nodded. "We'll take that with us."

Jamison didn't argue. This wasn't technically her scene to control so she'd leave the negotiation for evidence possession to Heather.

"Hey Shel. Take a look at this," Willie called from the door of George's closet.

Barrett crossed the room and looked into the closet.

"He's alerting on the shoes," Willie said.

"Okay. Let's bag them. Any other hits?"

"Nope."

Barrett turned to Terry. "Bag the laptop and anything else not nailed down. I'll be downstairs." She smiled at Jamison as she passed her. "Let's talk to Officer Cannon."

It sounded more like an order than an invitation but Jamison was finished in George's room anyway so she followed.

Heather sat beside Mrs. McGomery on the couch. She stood up as they entered, motioning them to follow her into the kitchen. "Did you find anything?"

"Got a hit on his shoes. Only residue but at least it's something," Barrett answered first.

Heather nodded, looking at Jamison. "Maybe we'll be able to tie him to the explosives you found."

Jamison leaned against the wall, taking the opportunity to join the conversation. "Maybe you can track the purchase of the Atlanta Wildcat ticket?" She addressed Barrett who now had possession of all evidence.

Barrett nodded and turned at footsteps sounding on the stairs. "I'll help the boys load everything and then bring you an evidence receipt." Without waiting for a response, she followed the other two agents out of the house.

"She either wasn't going to mention the ticket or she didn't see the connection," Jamison said softly. "I took a photo and already sent it to Todd. I want to know who he was sitting with."

Heather nodded. "Did I see a laptop as they passed?"

"You did. There wasn't much of anything else in the room though."

"Let's get out of here."

She met Agent Barrett at the door and took the evidence receipt. She explained to Mrs. McGomery what they had taken and left her a copy of the receipt. Jamison waited by the door, watching the agents secure items in their vehicle. When Heather finished they crossed to her sedan and climbed inside.

As soon as the doors closed Jamison spoke. "We know he had his hands on explosives so if not here at his house then where?" Jamison didn't wait for an answer from Heather but dialed Todd immediately.

"We need another location where this guy might have messed with the explosives. Maybe a storage building?" Jamison suggested.

"I already checked that. There's nothing in his name. No house, rental or storage building. Oh wait…his mother has a storage rental at Big Kings on Capital Circle southwest. It's their smallest available."

"I can call the judge and get him to do a verbal adjustment to the warrant based on the evidence already found." Heather picked up the phone and dialed.

Jamison took Todd off speaker while Heather talked with the judge. "Todd, have you found any connection between Hughes and Thomas?"

"Yeah, yeah," Todd said clearly distracted. "They served in the same unit in Vietnam. I tried to get phone records coming out of the Militia's compound but the Feds have that pretty sealed up. I couldn't find a cell phone for George McGomery either."

"I think Heather's going back in to talk with Mrs. McGomery so I'll have her ask about a cell phone."

Heather nodded and climbed out of the car.

Jamison disconnected her call and leaned her head against the seat. She thought about sending a text to Shea but didn't want to wake her. She hoped Shea had gotten comfortable with Liam and had been able to relax.

* * *

"That was a great movie," Shea said, standing. "I need to go to bed."

"Big game on Saturday, right?" Liam asked, the first hint that he knew who she was.

Shea smiled. "Something like that."

"I haven't lived in town long so I'm a Tennessee fan but since their season is already finished I was planning on rooting for the hometown team."

"That's very kind of you. Thanks for the pizza and the movie," Shea said over her shoulder as she entered the bedroom and closed the door.

She leaned against the closed door and stared at Jamison's room. The hunter green comforter made the small dark room feel more like a cave. The bathroom was larger than she expected with a walk-in shower and Jacuzzi tub. She pulled open every drawer and was pleased to find a brand-new toothbrush. She brushed her teeth and then took a shower, letting the hot water warm her body. She missed Jamison and realized this was the first time in four days they had been apart.

Thoughts of Jamison morphed into thoughts of Jamison naked in the shower. She longed to kiss her again. She wondered where Jamison might be right now and if they had caught the guy. Could all of this be over tonight? And if it was would she ever see Jamison again? Her arousal dissipated as she thought about not having Jamison in her life. Could she turn pro and still have a relationship with Jamison? She climbed out of the shower and dried herself on a thick mint green towel. Hanging the towel on the rack beside Jamison's she walked naked into the bedroom and began combing through the drawers in Jamison's dresser. She found a soft T-shirt and tossed it on the bed in case she woke up cold in the night. Underwear was a different issue so she decided to sleep without any.

She opened the bedroom door a crack, allowing a small amount of light to stream in. She hoped Jamison would return soon and maybe with the door open she would hear her. She smiled as she pulled Jamison's sheets around her naked body. The soft sound from the television soothed her, making her feel less alone, and she drifted off to sleep with thoughts of Jamison's reaction to finding her naked in her bed.

CHAPTER FIFTEEN

Heather slid back into the car. "She says we're welcome to search the storage unit." Heather shrugged. "Which wasn't a necessity since the judge cleared it too but now we have the key."

Suddenly the back door opened and Agent Sheldon Barrett slid in leaving the door hanging open.

"Where are we headed, ladies?" Sheldon asked with a smile.

Jamison remained quiet allowing Heather to answer with whatever information she wanted to share.

"Mrs. McGomery rents a storage unit on Capital Circle." Heather turned in her seat to make eye contact with Barrett. "We thought we would check it out. What plans do you guys have?"

"Nothing at the moment but if you don't mind we'd like to tag along. No need to send the dog back so soon." She started to slide out of the car and then paused. "What about his work office?"

Heather frowned. "I'm not sure the judge will go for that unless we can make a connection."

Barrett nodded. "Okay. How's this for a connection? The explosives found at Ms. Carter's house last night were tied to the mail bombs outside Atlanta two years ago."

"The FBI suspected the Mountain Militia for those bombings, right?" Heather asked excitedly.

Barrett nodded. "Suspected. Nothing solid."

Jamison shifted in her seat so she could see Barrett as well. "We were able to connect Charles Hughes and Clayton Thomas through their military service in Vietnam."

"I can work with this." Heather picked up her phone. "Let's see what the judge is willing to allow."

Jamison placed her hand on Heather's arm to stop her. "Did you ask if George had a cell phone?"

"Oh, right." Heather pulled a piece of paper from her pocket and passed it to Jamison. "Can you have Todd trace that? You'll probably be faster than the station would be."

Jamison called Todd and gave him the number while Heather contacted the judge.

Barrett waited silently until both had completed their calls.

"The judge says no right now but he said to call him back after we search the storage area and he might feel differently," Heather said, turning in her seat to face them. "Do you want to work some magic on your end, Agent Barrett?"

"I can see what I can do." She slid from the car and walked away with her phone pressed to her ear.

"I think the judge might be friends with Charles Hughes," Heather said, glancing at Jamison.

"That would explain his hesitancy."

"Yeah, he seemed surprised when I mentioned his connection to Clayton Thomas."

"Do you think she's coming back or should we just head to the storage unit?" Jamison asked, watching Barrett pace the sidewalk.

Heather shrugged. "She seems okay, right?"

"Well." Jamison laughed. "She seems nice enough but she's not very talkative."

"Typical."

They watched Barrett as she pocketed her phone and crossed to talk with the two FBI guys before heading back toward them.

"Let's go, ladies," Barrett said as she settled into the backseat of Heather's car.

Heather shrugged and put the car in gear. Heather radioed dispatch of their destination as well as who was accompanying her.

Jamison's cell rang and she placed Todd on speaker. "You're on speaker. Officer Cannon and FBI Special Agent Barrett are with me."

"And the party continues to grow," Todd said cheerily. "Good news. It was not a burn phone so I have call logs and text messages."

"That was quick," Barrett mumbled from the backseat.

"Yes, Special Agent Barrett, we are quick," Todd said.

Barrett raised her eyebrows and Jamison gave her shrug. "Tell us what you got, Todd."

"A lot of vague text messages that I'll tie to times and dates of the attacks and a few calls from an unknown number in Georgia. I'm still tracing it."

Though Todd couldn't see her Jamison narrowed her eyes. None of that information warranted an update. "Why did you call, Todd?"

"I have the name of Mr. McGomery's seat companion at the Atlanta game." He hesitated. "Well, I have the name of the person who purchased the tickets anyway."

She glanced at Heather and Barrett. "Continue."

"They're season tickets held by Clayton Thomas. I have it from a reliable source that Mr. Thomas doesn't miss a game but I'm scanning the cameras in that area of the stadium. I'll let you know when I confirm."

He disconnected and Barrett was the first to break the silence. "That's connection number two to the Mountain Militia."

"Why would the Mountain Militia care about a football game?" Jamison asked.

"They might not but season ticket holder, Clayton Thomas, might," Heather explained.

Jamison shook her head. "That seems crazy to me. Are people that crazy about a football game?"

"Some are even crazier," Heather said as she pulled up to the security punch pad in front of Big King's Storage. She entered the code Mrs. McGomery had given her and then pulled through the open gate. She turned to the right following the rows of storage units. "Three zero one. Mrs. McGomery said it was an end unit."

"Did she mention what she was storing?" Jamison asked.

"She said it had stuff left to her by her parents but she hadn't been in it in years."

"There it is." Jamison pointed and Heather stopped the car.

She pulled her pistol and covered Heather as she unlocked the unit.

Heather stepped inside and Jamison followed. After a quick scan with her flashlight, Jamison holstered her weapon and located the light switch.

"I don't think we need the bomb dog," Jamison said as she scanned a table stacked with explosives.

Barrett touched her arm. "Let Willie make sure nothing is wired and then we can look around."

Jamison and Heather followed her back outside while Willie and his dog entered the unit. Jamison dialed Todd.

"Get camera footage for Big King's Storage. Third row, end unit number three zero one. Find out who's been in this unit. We have explosives and I'm not sure what else."

"Do you need Kinsey to come back out?" Todd asked.

"No, we have an FBI bomb team with us."

"Okay. I'll start checking the footage."

Heather and Barrett were watching her. "Todd's going to check the camera footage here." She pointed to a camera above them. "Should have a good view."

"I don't think I'm needed here so I'm going to head back to the station and talk with Mr. McGomery." Heather looked at Jamison. "Want a ride?"

"Yep. I'm ready too."

From the car Jamison watched Heather exchange contact information with Barrett. She liked Heather's intense focus on the case and Barrett was growing on her too. Both stood at the same height but Barrett's dark features were a definitive contrast to Heather's fair complexion and blond hair. To her, the way they stood relaxed and talking while still aware of their surroundings, both women were easily identifiable as law enforcement officers.

Heather slid into the car and radioed dispatch she was turning the scene over to the FBI and heading back to the station. When she returned the microphone to its holder she glanced at Jamison. "Do you want me to drop you off?"

Jamison sighed. "I guess so. I should pick up my truck at Shea's so we aren't stranded tomorrow."

Heather radioed dispatch of her detour and then turned toward campus. "There's no doubt McGomery is our guy."

"I can't argue with that."

"The FBI will be the rest of the night processing that scene at the storage unit. Who knows what all they'll find."

Jamison rubbed her face. "Do you really think McGomery is smart enough to make a bomb?"

"Maybe not since he didn't really make one, did he?"

"So you think he purchased all the pieces but didn't know how to put it together?"

"Why not? He wanted to stop the Tigers from playing, not necessarily hurt or kill anyone." Heather pulled to a stop behind Jamison's truck. "I'll call you tomorrow morning and let you know what McGomery has to say. Maybe we'll get a search warrant for his office by then too though it seems we already found his workshop." She paused. "I think I'll call the judge and get the warrant to cover McGomery's entire house. I'd like to see that spare bedroom and since the rental unit was in his mother's name I don't think I'll have a problem."

Jamison nodded and climbed out of the car. "Keep in touch."

Heather pulled away from the curb leaving Jamison standing in the glow from the streetlight. She glanced at Shea's empty duplex. Why had McGomery taken his love of football to this level? Jamison was sure someone else had encouraged him or maybe even assisted him. She was eager to find out where McGomery had managed to get his explosives and supplies but for now she only wanted to tell Shea it was over.

CHAPTER SIXTEEN

Shea's eyes flew open at the sound of the front door closing. She heard the murmur of voices coming from the living room and then the front door closed again. She was alone with Jamison. Her pulse raced as the lights in the apartment disappeared one at a time and then footsteps sounded outside the bedroom door. After a few moments of watching Jamison's shadow in the doorway, she rolled onto her side and leaned on one elbow holding the comforter across her bare chest. "Are you coming in?"

Jamison crossed the room and sat on the edge of the bed. "I didn't think you were awake."

She took Jamison's hand, running her fingers across her palm and up the inside of her arm. "I was waiting for you. What time is it?"

"After midnight. I'm sorry it's so late. We caught a lead and followed it."

"Did you catch him?"

Jamison stroked her thumb across the back of Shea's hand. "Yes. He's in custody."

She could hear the hesitation in Jamison's voice but she wasn't going to pursue it tonight. All she heard was that it was over.

Jamison's fingertips stroked her naked shoulder. "Didn't I mention there were clothes in the dresser?"

"You might have."

Jamison's fingers drifted down her arm and then back up to her neck playing with strands of hair.

"I need a shower." Jamison stood and pointed across the room. "That's the only one in the apartment. Will it bother you?"

"Will it bother you if I join you?"

* * *

Jamison's breath caught. *Yes, yes, yes.* She wanted Shea's body in her arms. She had been telling herself no for so long that her mind continued to taunt her. *I can't do this.* She pushed the thoughts away. The case was over. She couldn't fight against something she wanted so badly. She stared openly as Shea pushed the covers back exposing her naked body. She led her into the bathroom and turned on the water, undressing under Shea's watchful gaze. Her body quivered at Shea's touch and she pulled away, stepping into the shower.

Under the spray, she groaned as the full length of Shea's naked body pressed against her own. She kissed Shea's neck and found her soft lips, deepening the kiss. Her hands and mouth explored Shea's body and she lost herself in the fire raging inside her. She easily released her control and let Shea take the lead. Shea pulled their bodies hard together as her lips returned to Jamison's mouth again and again. She wrapped her arms around Shea's neck and held on to her shoulders. The pace Shea set was fast and Jamison surrendered quickly.

Shea turned off the water and pulled two towels from the rack. Jamison wrapped the towel around her body and leaned against Shea.

"We need to move to the bed."

"That's exactly what I was thinking."

She slid her hand into Shea's and followed her into the bedroom.

She had never shared her bed with anyone before. She purposely kept a single bed in her room for that reason. It was not an invitation for someone to spend the night. She lay sideways resting on her elbow with half her body stretched across Shea.

Shea breathed softly into her ear. "Don't look so tired. I'm not finished with you yet."

Jamison groaned. "Don't you need your rest?"

"Not yet. Right now I need more of you."

She stroked Shea's face.

With an arm around Shea's waist, she savored the feel of Shea's skin beneath her fingertips. She rolled onto her back and slid behind her. Moving her hand lightly across Shea's stomach, she traced a path down her thigh. She pulled Shea's leg across her body and slowly followed the muscle up until her fingers found what they desired. Shea's back lay flat against her chest and she slid her left arm around her neck, running her hand across Shea's chest. She teased each nipple, making Shea moan and push her body tighter against hers. Shea lifted her arms above her head, giving her entire body to Jamison. They moved together as one and she whispered softly in Shea's ear until she felt her body release.

* * *

Jamison awoke as the sun seeped in around the curtains. She lay on her back with Shea in her arms, one hand cupping Shea's breast, the other across her hip. She didn't remember falling asleep and hoped that she hadn't been mid-stroke when it happened. She smiled. It didn't matter. If she had, she would make it up to her. The muscles in her arms and legs ached but the rest of her screamed for more of Shea.

She rolled Shea onto her side and left her curled in a ball, sleeping. In the shower she kept the water cool, trying to slow down her racing libido. She wanted to blame her reaction to Shea on her lack of sex but she knew deep down she had never felt passion like that with anyone before. Shea was an amazing woman. She was intelligent and interesting with a body sculpted from years of workouts. Jamison knew she would never be able to rid her memory of Shea's long muscular legs wrapped around her body.

Even now, hours later, she could close her eyes and feel Shea's body moving beneath her. Soft skin over hard muscle. Jamison leaned against the shower wall smacking her head several times against the tile. For all the talk she had heard over the years about taking a cold shower, clearly they didn't work as prescribed. Standing under the cold spray, she quickly realized not thinking about Shea was not going to be an option. Her mind and her body were both wrapped around her and she wanted to embrace the wonderful feeling instead of continuing to fight it. She was tired of fighting it. She wanted Shea in her life, and with the case over, her path was clear to do all the things she had resisted over the last week.

In the light of the kitchen, her hazy dream state turned to the events of the night before she came home to Shea. Could McGomery really be working alone? If not, then who else was involved? And why? Picking up her cell phone, she hoped Heather wasn't sleeping because she needed an update.

Heather answered on the first ring.

"What's the news?" she asked, adding water to the coffeemaker.

"I've just spent the last five hours processing the McGomery's house. Seems there was a shed out back where Georgie kept his bicycle that Mom forgot to mention the first or second time we were there."

"Find anything good?"

"Oh yeah. Instruction manuals on everything from building a bomb to proper placement to bring down a building. We even found a manual on how to install new brakes on a bus." Heather paused. "Oh yeah, and we brought his mother into the station for questioning. I don't think she had anything to do with this but it's her house and she had to hear or see something."

Jamison moaned as strong arms wrapped around her waist and Shea's lips grazed her neck. She turned and pulled Shea tight against her body, clearing her throat to cover the moan. "Okay then."

Heather chuckled. "Guess I don't have to ask what you did after we parted last night. Did you at least get out of bed before you called me?"

Jamison turned in Shea's arms, ignoring Heather's harassment. "What's the plan now?"

"I'm headed back to the station to begin mounds of paperwork and then I'm going to make another run at Georgie. Maybe bringing his mother in will work something loose in him."

Jamison moaned again when Shea's fingers found a tight spot in her back.

"Hey lover girl. In case you forgot some of us have been up all night and are still working," Heather teased. "Can you focus for a minute?"

"Sorry," Jamison mumbled, stepping out of Shea's reach. "Can you have Todd send me the cell phone information he ran last night?"

"Sure. I'll call him right now."

"Yeah, right. Just before noon if you can. Oh, and you better move away from that woman when you make the call."

Jamison laughed and pulled the phone from her ear. Heather had disconnected without a good-bye.

"Did she hang up on you?" Shea asked.

"Kind of. She's not really into long good-byes." Jamison dialed Flagler. She didn't expect that Todd would still be on shift but they would get a message to him.

"He's asleep in the briefing room but he said to wake him if you called." Jamison was advised.

"No, just give him the message. It's not urgent so he can call me when he wakes up."

She tossed her cell phone on the counter and pulled Shea into her arms. "I hope last night is not going to affect your performance tomorrow."

Shea kissed her nose. "You don't need to worry about my performance." She kissed both sides of Jamison's mouth and then connected fully with her lips. She broke the kiss and sniffed the air. "Is that coffee?"

"Yep."

Jamison scrambled eggs and they ate as they discussed their day. She was glad she had brought the truck back last night.

"We need to get going soon or you'll be late for class."

Shea wrinkled her nose. "I don't want to go to class."

Jamison smiled. "Isn't there a rule about skipping class and you can't play tomorrow?"

"Argh." Shea took a sip of her coffee. "Maybe Coach will clear me after the night I had."

Jamison raised her eyebrows.

Shea lightly kicked her under the table. "I didn't mean that. I'll tell him about the break-in."

"I should call Chief Hammer too." Jamison released a breath. "Though I'm not sure what to say."

Shea frowned. "You made an arrest, right? So, it's over."

"Heather made an arrest, yes, but it's only over if he was working alone."

"Well, crap." Shea lightly kicked her again. "You don't think he was, do you?"

Jamison grimaced and shook her head.

"What does Heather think?"

"She thinks sometimes you take what you can get."

"What does that mean?"

Jamison lifted her mug of coffee and took a sip while she chose her words. She wished she hadn't started this conversation with Shea. She wanted her focused on the game and not worried about what might be.

"It means as a cop sometimes she can't get the person calling the shots so she settles for the case she can prove."

"So you both think someone else is calling the shots here?"

Jamison shrugged and placed her cup on the table. "Let's take one thing at a time."

She picked up her phone and dialed Coach Sutton. She gave him a brief summary of the night's activities and asked if he thought it would be okay if Shea skipped class today. He agreed to contact her professors and if there was a problem he would call back.

"He's okay with you skipping class but wants you at practice. Just a walk-through and some stretching though."

"Friday practices are normally pretty light." Shea wrinkled her brow.

"What's wrong?"

"I wish I had the DVD with my film footage from the house."

Jamison smiled. "I'd have mentioned that I grabbed it last night if you hadn't distracted me as soon as I got here."

"That's great! Thanks." Shea stood. "So that's what you older folks call it. A distraction?" She darted out of Jamison's grasp and called over her shoulder. "I'm taking a shower. Distractions are welcome."

She considered following Shea but picked up her phone instead. Unfortunately she still had people to update. She dialed the Tallahassee University security department. "Chief Hammer, please."

"Hey Jamison. How's our cub?"

Jamison smiled. In the beginning, Shea was his cub and now he was sharing her. She knew how much Shea meant to him and was pleased he seemed to think she was worthy of protecting Shea. "She's doing okay. Did Coach already call you?"

"I just hung up with him."

"I'm sorry, Chief. I should've called you first. Shea wanted to get cleared from her classes today and Coach has that magic power."

"It's no problem. Can I ask who the guy was though?"

"I'm surprised his arrest didn't make the morning papers. George McGomery."

Carlton was silent.

"Ring any bells?"

"Unfortunately, I can't say that it does. What do we know about him?"

"He's a local boy. Works at Watson-Hughes, a small data processing company on Thomasville Road. Still lives at home with his mother and is an Atlanta Wildcats fan."

Carlton groaned. "One of those guys. No wonder he hates the Tigers."

"Is that a big rivalry?"

"Not in the past but it's clear we have to go through them to get to the National Championship. They've won the last three years and it's rumored their coach is about to take an NFL job."

"Wow. Would a loss cost him the job?"

"Probably. Not too many make the jump from college ball to the pros."

"That's something to think about."

"I'll see you this afternoon?" Carlton asked.

"Yep. I'll be there."

Jamison dropped onto the couch and tossed her cell phone on the coffee table. She could make the leap from George McGomery through Charles Hughes to Clayton Thomas but not to the Atlanta Wildcats' coach. George McGomery had all the makings of a white supremacist psychopath but he would need help and direction from someone with more power. Clayton Thomas definitely fit that bill. Did he love the Wildcats enough to jeopardize his law-abiding militia group, though?

"Hey." Shea dropped onto the couch beside Jamison. "I thought you were going to join me?"

"Sorry." She smiled and pulled Shea into her arms. "I got sidetracked."

Shea kissed her neck and bit her shoulder. "Distractions and sidetracked. When will it just be about me?" she pouted.

Jamison gave her a quick kiss.

"It's always about you, baby," she said. "Now we'll watch football. There'll be no touching for the remainder of the day."

"What?"

"I refuse to be the reason you can't perform tomorrow."

"Abstaining before a game is a hoax," she heard Shea yell as she walked into the bedroom to dress for the day.

CHAPTER SEVENTEEN

Jamison covered her gently with the soft blanket from the back of the couch. Shea stirred and opened her eyes. "How long was I asleep?"

"About an hour."

Shea got up and retrieved a bottle of water from the refrigerator, then dropped back down on the couch. "Do you have any tea? I'm a little chilled."

Jamison put water on to boil and walked back into the living room. Shea was curled under the blanket. She touched her forehead and frowned. "You're warm."

"It's probably lack of sleep. I sometimes run a fever when I'm tired."

Jamison returned to the kitchen and switched tea bags to non-caffeinated. Shea needed rest, not caffeine. She returned to the living room with two ibuprofen and handed them to Shea. She was surprised when Shea didn't question her and took the two pills. While she waited for the tea to steep, she placed the game footage disc in the player and grabbed another blanket from her bedroom closet. She handed Shea the remote control and her cup of tea, sliding in behind her on the couch. She wrapped both arms around her and cocooned their bodies with the blankets.

Shea hit play on the DVD player and they watched in silence. It wasn't long before Shea drifted off to sleep again. Jamison watched the footage, making mental notes on what she wanted to mention to Shea when she woke up.

Jamison awoke several hours later when Shea began to stir. Shea sat up and turned to look at Jamison. "Were you sleeping too?"

She nodded and picked up her phone from the coffee table. Shea smiled when she ordered a large supreme pizza and a salad.

Thirty minutes later the downstairs door buzzed and Shea jumped to her feet. "Pizza!"

Jamison pushed her back on the couch and walked to the kitchen. "Stay there." She pushed the intercom button. "Yes."

"Pizza delivery."

"Come on up." Jamison pressed the door release and looked at Shea. "What the hell?"

"Was that Heather?"

Jamison nodded and opened the door checking the empty hall before walking to the glass elevator foyer. She glanced back at Shea who had followed her and pointed a finger at her. Without a word, Shea stepped back inside the apartment pushing the door partially closed but still looking out. Jamison smiled. Shea was still following her instructions without question where safety was concerned.

The elevator doors opened and Heather stepped out carrying their order.

"Take up a new part-time job?" Jamison asked, opening the foyer door allowing her to exit.

Heather gave her a half smile. "I didn't mean to interrupt your lunch but the delivery guy arrived at the same time. Can I come in for a second? I need to talk to you."

"Sure. How'd you find us?" Jamison took the pizza from her arms and led the way into the apartment. Shea had retreated to the couch but Jamison knew she was still within hearing range. She dropped the pizza box on the table and leaned against the counter, facing Heather.

"Todd told me." Heather surveyed the apartment, giving Shea a wave, and then dropped her voice. "I didn't get to grill McGomery again."

"Why not?"

Heather looked at Shea and then back at Jamison.

"Shea?" Jamison nodded toward the bedroom. Heather seemed uncomfortable continuing the conversation with Shea in the room.

Shea stood and faced them, but her eyes were on Jamison. "I want to hear what she has to say."

Jamison stared into her face. She wanted her to be safe. No, she *needed* her to be safe but she knew that look of determination. This was not a battle she would win. She turned back to Heather. "What happened?"

"McGomery was released."

"What?" she and Shea said in unison.

Jamison said to Heather, "Was it a mix-up? Someone screwed up?" She expected FBI interference but the last thing she imagined was McGomery back on the street.

"No, his bail was posted." Heather sighed and sank into a chair at the table. "But he shouldn't have even had bail set yet. I'd have held him a while longer before taking him in front of a judge, and with what we found at his house and the storage unit we probably could've gotten the judge to refuse bail." She kicked her legs out in front of her and leaned back into the chair, exhaustion showing on her face. "I don't understand. It feels like someone's working behind our backs to undercut us. His bail was paid in cash and no one got a good look at the man that paid it."

Shea pulled three beers from the refrigerator and set them on the table along with a stack of paper plates. She sat down across from Heather and twisted the cap off a bottle, taking a long drink. Jamison handed Heather a bottle of water and replaced Shea's beer as well.

Grabbing a slice of pizza, Shea frowned at Jamison. "So, this idiot is back on the street now?"

Heather opened a beer and took a drink. "I'm afraid so."

Jamison wanted more information but was hesitant to expose her thoughts in front of Shea. Trying to hide the anger and fear in her voice, she said. "With what was found in the storage unit and in his house on the second search can't you arrest him on different charges?"

Nodding, Heather helped herself to two slices of pizza. "I got an arrest warrant but he didn't go back to his house."

"He probably went to the compound in Atlanta with his militia buddy that bailed him out." Jamison shook her head.

Shea jumped on Jamison's words. "Militia!"

Crap. Jamison placed a hand on Shea's arm. She had forgotten Shea didn't know any details from last night. "The explosives have been tied to a bombing in Atlanta from a couple of years ago. The FBI believe the Mountain Militia were responsible but they couldn't connect them enough for any arrests."

"So you think this McGomery guy is tied to the Mountain Militia?" Shea looked at Jamison and then Heather. Her dark eyes drilling both of them.

Heather finished her bite of pizza, then said, "We aren't sure about anything yet, Ms. Carter. It's still under investigation."

"That's the crappy line you give other people. I want to know what you guys think," Shea demanded.

Heather shrugged at Jamison, allowing her to decide what information to share with Shea.

Jamison waited until Shea's eyes found hers again. "Shea, you need to concentrate on the game and let us worry about what's happening off the field."

"Yeah, well, that's kinda hard to do." Shea stood up and went to the couch. She hit play on the DVD player but didn't turn up the volume.

Jamison knew she was listening and couldn't blame her. It was her life at risk and though Shea trusted her she still wanted to know what was going on. She leaned toward Heather. "What's the FBI saying about this?"

"Wallace was gone when I returned to the station and he hasn't returned my call yet. I was thinking about calling Barrett and see if she would talk to me."

Jamison nodded. "Call her now. See if she'll come here."

Heather pulled her phone from her pocket and dialed.

Jamison walked over and sat beside Shea. "Are you okay?" she asked softly.

Shea shrugged and continue to watch the television screen.

"Shea?"

"What? What do you want me to say?" She looked at Jamison. "A lunatic is out to get me and I just found out he might be joined by a militia."

Jamison touched her arm. "I'm going to keep you safe."

Shea's eyes softened as they searched Jamison's face. "I believe that, Jamison. I do. I just don't understand why he's back on the street already."

Jamison glanced at Heather who was stuffing her phone back in her pocket. She squeezed Shea's arm. "Neither do I but I'm going to find out. Okay?"

Shea nodded.

Heather ate the last bite of her pizza and tossed the empty box on the counter by the trash can. "Barrett's on her way. She was her usual chatty self on the phone so I'm not sure what she'll share with us."

"Who's Barrett?" Shea asked.

"FBI. She was with us last night when we searched McGomery's house," Jamison answered, motioning for Heather to join them on the couch. "Did she know McGomery had been released?"

Heather shrugged. "She didn't say either way but I don't think she did."

Twenty minutes later when the doorbell buzzed Shea and Heather were deep in a discussion about game strategy. Jamison went to the intercom and buzzed Barrett into the building.

Barrett, dressed in her FBI-issued black suit, greeted Jamison with a handshake when she opened the elevator foyer door. Leading the way into the apartment, Jamison was surprised to see Heather waiting by the door. Removing her hand from her weapon, she gave Barrett a nod and then returned to her conversation with Shea. Jamison was pleased to see Heather's reaction to protecting Shea even though she knew the glass doors surrounding the elevator were bulletproof. Her apartment had been used as a safe house for a period of time. Flagler had several around the city and once they were no longer usable they were rented out to employees.

"Cannon, you going to join us today?" Jamison interrupted Heather's conversation with Shea.

"Shea Carter," Shea said, stepping forward and offering her hand to Barrett.

"Sheldon Barrett. It's nice to finally meet you, Ms. Carter. And please, it's Sheldon," she said, looking at all three women.

Jamison offered seats at the kitchen table and briefly stroked Shea's back as she passed. She wouldn't embarrass Shea again by asking her to leave the room, but hoped she would do it willingly. She saw Shea smile when she caught Sheldon watching their interaction. She studied Sheldon's face but saw only curiosity in her reaction. She waited until Shea was settled on the couch, pretending to focus on the television, before turning to the women across from her.

"How can I help you, ladies?" Sheldon asked, getting right to the point.

Jamison glanced at Heather and then asked. "What can you tell us about the mail bombings two years ago?"

Clearly that wasn't the question Sheldon had expected and she took a while before answering. "Two families received packages in their home mailboxes. Neither package actually traveled through the postal system but were placed after the mail had been deposited in the box. The first one was picked up by the official's son when he got home from school."

"Right." Heather nodded. "He was only ten and luckily it didn't go off like it was supposed to when the package was moved."

"He made it inside the house and dropped it on the kitchen counter." Sheldon continued. "His mother arrived right behind him as she had been the intended target and normally picked up the mail each day."

"Who was she?" Jamison asked.

"She was and still is a prosecuting attorney for the State of Georgia. At the time, she was assisting the sheriff's department in compiling a case against the Mountain Militia. None of this information was ever released to the public and the case is still ongoing. The sheriff's department had intercepted a shipment of guns by accident and almost had the truck driver singing like a canary. He was a third striker and willing to do anything to stay out of prison. This was the first time he'd ever done a job for the Mountain Militia and didn't know how far they could reach."

Jamison leaned forward. "I was overseas at the time and I barely remember when this happened. If they had this guy, what happened?"

Sheldon shrugged. "The second bomb was in the mailbox of the trucker's family. When his wife opened the box it detonated killing her and their one-year-old son she held in her arms."

"Oh shit," Jamison whispered.

"Two different militia groups claimed responsibility for the attacks but neither was the Mountain Militia," Heather added.

Sheldon nodded. "Right. We believe Clayton Thomas worked out a deal with the other groups to pull the heat from his organization. The guy offered up as the ringleader was a nobody who'd been in and out of prison too many times to count. He was prosecuted but everyone knew he wasn't the person responsible. We thought what happened would make the trucker angry and he'd agree to help us, but the militia got to him first threatening his mother and father as well as the rest of his family. He clammed up and took his third strike." Sheldon sighed. "Not that it mattered because he was killed in a prison fight a couple of months later."

"What's the group's mission?" Jamison asked, looking between Heather and Sheldon.

Heather jumped in. "That's the thing. We don't think they have one. They seem to only want to stay off the government radar and live in their little commune."

Sheldon nodded. "Most militia groups have a mission and a plan of attack. They're after someone or a group that represents something. The Mountain Militia are preparing for the day when our government will fall."

"Which is why they're stockpiling weapons and apparently explosives," Jamison stated, shaking her head. "Then why are they coming out of the woodwork now? Can Clayton Thomas really be that crazy about football that's he's willing to risk everything he's put together?"

"It doesn't seem likely." Heather shook her head. "But yet, there's definitely a connection."

Jamison sat back in her chair. "Maybe McGomery was really acting alone."

Heather looked at Sheldon. "Did Agent Wallace get anything out of him before he was released?"

"Wallace couldn't get him to admit anything more than he placed the explosives. He claimed everything in the storage locker was his and he worked alone."

"So where did he get the explosives?" Jamison asked.

Sheldon shook her head. "He claims he drove to Miami and picked them up from a guy he didn't know. No name, no description and he changed the date he supposedly made the drive several times." She looked at Jamison and Heather. "By the way, Wallace had already left TPD when McGomery was taken before the judge. I called him after you told me what happened and he had no idea."

Jamison's cell phone buzzed with a text message. "It's Todd," she said, looking up from her phone. "He says it's urgent."

"Todd?" Sheldon asked.

"Todd is the magic worker at Flagler. He can make information appear from thin air," Heather explained.

"Right, I remember him from last night." Sheldon nodded. "Let's hear what the magic man has to say."

Jamison dialed Flagler. "Hey Todd. You're on speaker with the whole gang. What's up?"

"Officer Cannon gave me access to TPD's surveillance cameras this morning so I've been trying to identify the man who posted McGomery's bail. He's Daryl Kincaid. Nothing in the system for him except a driver's license. His residence is the Mountain Militia compound. About an hour ago, McGomery's phone was turned back on and I'm tracking him headed north on Interstate Seventy-Five."

"He's headed to the militia compound then," Jamison stated.

"That's what I assume too and I'll let you know when he arrives at his destination. In other news, I ran a financial check on Watson-Hughes and they're having trouble paying their bills and employee paychecks. Which seemed odd to me with the amount of money moving through the company so I dug a little deeper. It seems the bulk of their income is coming from one company and I'm having trouble finding an owner's name for it. I've been tracking it through one shell company after another."

"That sounds like a job for my department. Can you email me all the details, Todd?" Sheldon gave him her email address.

"Everything I've dug up is on its way to you now, Agent Barrett," Todd said. "And now for McGomery." He paused and they listened to clicking as his fingers flew over the keyboard. "He made two calls. One to his mother's home number. It only lasted a few seconds. The second call was to the same number from Atlanta he was calling before you arrested him. I can't tie this number to a person. Only to a company and it's one of the companies Watson-Hughes has been taking money from. That phone hasn't been turned on since I started trying to track it last night but when McGomery called it we were able to come up with a general location—" He broke off.

"Todd?" Jamison spoke softly.

"Just a second. One of my techs has something."

Jamison watched Sheldon flip through the emails Todd had sent her on her phone. She exchanged a glance with Heather but no one spoke as they waited. Out of the corner of her eye, she could see Shea watching her with acute interest and she gave her a quick smile.

"Okay." Todd said, coming back on the line. "The general location for the other phone is outside Atlanta in the mountains. I'm going to take a wild guess and pin that as the location of the Mountain Militia compound. Now for the update on McGomery's phone. It's been turned off now but we were able to track it to the same location."

"McGomery is at the militia compound." Heather repeated what Todd had said, letting it sink in. She looked at Sheldon. "Let's go get him."

Sheldon sat back in her chair. "I'm listening. What do you propose?"

"Let's just drive up to the gate and see if they'll turn him over. If they want to claim they're law abiding then they will."

"What are you going to charge him with?" Sheldon asked.

"Illegal possession of explosives. His mother signed a sworn statement that the explosives in the storage unit weren't hers and that George was the only other person with access to it. I issued the warrant before I left the station."

"I have footage of George entering the storage facility several times in the last week," Todd added.

"I'm good with it." She looked at Jamison. "Are you in?"

"No," she said without hesitation, glancing at Shea. "I need to stay with Shea until you guys get him in custody again." She lowered her voice. "Besides, we can't be sure someone else won't pick up where McGomery left off."

Sheldon nodded. "We plan to have agents inside the stadium tomorrow as well as bomb dogs."

"TPD will have a strong presence too," Heather added. She looked at Sheldon. "How many dogs do you have? Can we get one for every entrance?"

Sheldon shrugged. "How many are you talking?"

Heather looked at Jamison for confirmation. "Maybe four or five?"

"I'll have to check on that."

"I bet Kinsey and Jack would be willing to help out too," Jamison added.

"I'll call her now," Todd chimed in. "I'll call if I get anything else." He clicked off.

"I have the stadium plans," Jamison said. "Let's iron down a few details in case I don't get to talk with you guys again before the game."

* * *

Shea stared at the three women sitting at the table, their heads bent in intense conversation. Heather and Sheldon were beautiful women but they didn't have Jamison's rogue exterior. Jamison didn't have to follow the rules though it seemed like she did anyway. No one told her what to do but she followed her conscience in making her decisions with integrity. Shea liked the determination she saw in Jamison's face to keep her safe. In her eyes, Jamison was the most attractive of the three and she watched the way her lips moved when she talked.

She couldn't remember ever wanting more of a woman and she couldn't wait to have her hands on Jamison again. She looked away when she caught Jamison's eye but quickly glanced back again. Jamison's attention was focused on what Sheldon was saying but her eyes seemed to caress Shea. She shivered and pulled the blanket around her, glancing one last time at Jamison before returning her gaze to the television. Jamison gave her a half smile, her focus still on the women at the table and Shea felt her stomach flutter. The way Jamison looked at her made her feel special. She knew at that moment that she would never be able to give Jamison up.

CHAPTER EIGHTEEN

Shea could feel Jamison's eyes on her. The silence in the truck felt heavy between them and she knew Jamison was concerned.

Sheldon had left for the FBI field office to make preparations to pick up McGomery and Heather was headed for TPD to get approval from Chief Stillwell to accompany Sheldon. They'd both assured Jamison they'd call with details as soon as a plan was created. She felt Jamison glance at her again.

"What?" she finally asked.

"You've been very quiet."

"I'm trying not to think about everything. I can't stop this guy or his friends so I have to leave it to you."

Jamison nodded. "We'll get him."

She was silent again as they turned into the stadium and Jamison parked the truck. A glimpse of the pistol Jamison carried made her stomach turn. An all-too-serious reminder of what she was facing. She watched Jamison climb out of the truck, look around and then walk around to her door. She didn't want to be dependent on anyone but Jamison's confidence was reassuring and she leaned into her as they walked toward the stadium.

"You'll stay close, right?"

Jamison's arm slid around her waist, holding her tight. "I'll be in the stands with Carlton."

Shea stopped and their eyes met.

"And I'll be watching you every second."

* * *

The locker room was quiet as Coach Sutton talked. Jamison looked slowly around the room taking in each player. Their faces were somber with none of the joking she had seen over the last few days.

"Hit the field and start your stretches. I'll be there shortly." Coach Sutton motioned everyone toward the door. "Agent Krews, can I speak with you?" He placed a hand on her arm as she passed.

Jamison hesitated. She needed to follow Shea but she hadn't missed the seriousness of his voice. "Can we talk on the field?"

Coach Sutton nodded. "Yeah, right. Let's talk while we walk."

They followed Shea and the team down the hallway.

Jamison gave him a minute to gather his thoughts and then she prompted him. "Everything okay, Coach?"

"I have a detective friend who works for TPD. He says the guy you arrested was released."

Jamison nodded. "George McGomery was arrested last night for breaking into Ms. Carter's house." She searched his face for any sign of recognition of the name. "He was picked up at his home with no problem but someone bailed him out this morning."

Coach Sutton frowned. "Someone?"

Jamison took a deep breath. "They avoided TPD cameras in the station and paid cash. They didn't want to be seen."

"So he has accomplices?"

Jamison stopped as they stepped onto the field her eyes on Shea. "TPD and the FBI are working together. I've met with them and I'm confident they'll uncover the truth. We have a plan for tomorrow's game so please don't let this distract you."

"I've been in football my entire life and have never experienced anything like this. I know people can get obsessed and fans can go a little crazy but this is beyond imagination. The conference is considering canceling the game. They're afraid something horrible might happen on national television."

"As I said before, TPD and the FBI are on top of this."

"We already have a no bags rule. It'd be hard for anyone to bring something in through the ticket gates unless it's strapped to their body."

"Right, so we're going to have bomb dogs at every entrance and plainclothes as well as uniformed officers everywhere. I'm going to get with Carlton right now and we'll have every access to the stadium monitored."

He nodded as he watched the team warm up. "They're a good bunch of kids and they deserve this win."

"And we're going to make sure they get the opportunity."

He nodded again as he walked away from her.

She sighed. She wished she felt as confident as she had sounded to him. Climbing the steps into the stands she dialed Todd. "How many agents can Flagler spare for tomorrow's game?"

"Mrs. Bowden and I have been working on that. We have about twenty-five locked in including Kinsey."

"That's great, Todd. Send me the list of names and I'll make sure security has their passes ready. Can you ask them to be on the north side of the stadium parking lot at zero nine? I'll provide diagrams of the stadium and coordinate their assignments. TPD and the FBI bomb teams are going to clear the entire stadium starting at zero six."

"I wish I could be there too," Todd said with regret. "Give Ms. Carter a good luck from us and we'll be watching on the big screen here in ops."

Jamison smiled, wondering if Bowden had approved the ops screen to be used for the game.

Reading her mind Todd added, "Mrs. Bowden is coming in too and she's bringing pizza."

"Wow," Jamison said, leaning against the metal bars separating the seats from the field. She allowed herself a moment to enjoy the support from her team.

Shea's voice echoed through the quiet stadium as she called the plays. Jamison climbed the remaining steps to join Carlton on the fifty-yard line.

"How's our cub today?"

"She's a little shaken up." Jamison filled him in on the events that had taken place after they spoke earlier.

His head bobbed as he nodded his acknowledgment but his eyes never left the team. "McGomery, huh? I'm sure I don't recognize the name. And he's a local?"

"Yep, still lives in his childhood home on Krest Street."

"And he's back on the street now," Carlton stated and Jamison could hear the unease in his voice.

"Hopefully not for long. The FBI will be on their way to pick him up shortly."

"So you know where he is?"

"We're tracking his phone."

Carlton's head bobbed again. "What can I do to help? I know TPD will start clearing the stadium at zero six."

"Yes, the TPD is coordinating with the FBI and they'll have bomb dogs for each ticket entrance. Flagler is sending twenty-five agents as well. I'll email you that list as soon as I get it. I'm briefing them at zero nine in the stadium parking lot on the north side if you want to send any of your officers too."

"I'll send a handful but the rest will already be on details. I'm briefing all of my officers tonight after practice if you want to attend."

"I'll do that." She pulled a notepad from her pocket. "Let's go over all vendors and anyone else that will have access to the stadium without passing through ticket entrances."

For the remainder of practice, she worked through details with Carlton for a plan they'd both be able to follow with their staff. When Shea trotted off the field, she waited at the tunnel entrance for Jamison and together they walked back into the locker room.

"Coach has film footage set up in his office…" Shea let her words hang.

"That's fine. Once you're settled there I'm going with Carlton to brief his staff." She glanced at Shea. "If you're okay with that?"

Shea nodded. "There'll be about five or six players and all the coaching staff with me. I'll wait there until you return though."

Jamison winked at her. "I'll come back for you as soon as I can."

* * *

Jamison studied her notepad trying not to think about Shea, naked, less than thirty feet away from her. She had specific points she needed Carlton to touch on to make sure his staff would be on the same page as everyone else. She glanced up at movement in the room and quickly looked back at her notepad making Shea laugh. Instead of wrapping her towel around her body, Shea was using it to dry her hair.

"Nice view," Jamison mumbled, refusing to look up again.

When Shea finally began pulling on clothes, Jamison risked another look. She could feel the velvety softness of the skin across Shea's back, remembering how her fingers had slid down to the curve of her hip. Jamison quickly stood, turning away from Shea. She needed to keep these images far away from her thoughts. She'd already decided she was sleeping on the couch tonight though she hadn't broken the news to Shea. She knew how her muscles ached this morning after their marathon last night and she didn't want anything holding Shea back tomorrow.

Shea crossed the room dressed in jeans and a long sleeved T-shirt. "Coach keeps his office in arctic temperatures year round. He says he's hot-blooded but I think he does it so no one will stay long."

"I remember that from the first day I was in there. I thought the cold was left from your exit."

Shea bumped her shoulder. "Nice one."

Together they walked down the hall. Returning to the administration portion of the stadium, she noticed Coach Sutton's door standing open.

"Good," Shea said softly. "Some of the cold is escaping."

Jamison laughed. "How long do you think you'll be here?"

"Probably an hour or so."

"Okay. I'll be back for you." She tapped her pocket. "If anything changes call me though."

Shea gave her a slim smile and walked into the office.

Jamison watched her until she took a seat on the leather sofa along with two other players, then turned to quickly cross the campus to the security office. The look Shea had given her before she left was piercing but there was something else in it. Something that made her feel warm inside and a little uncomfortable at the same time. She knew she was interested in pursuing more than a one-night stand with Shea but until now she hadn't really been sure what Shea was thinking.

Mel had told her during training that someone being protected could attach intimate feelings to their protector and she had even experienced such situations herself. However, remaining professional had been easy and had kept the situation clear. She had crossed too many lines to count with Shea and Mel was going to kill her. *Mel!* She hadn't briefed Mel today. She might be ready to kill her on more than one count now. Jamison's thoughts churned as she tried to think about how she would tell Mel how she felt about her sister. She climbed the steps to the security office thankful to find the meeting already in progress. There would be plenty of time later to think of the talk she needed to have with Mel.

Jamison followed the sound of voices coming from the rear of the building. She was surprised to see such a large number of people crammed inside the office. She leaned against the wall inside the door and Carlton gave her a nod. She counted over fifty men and women squished into every available chair and leaning against the walls. Several people glanced curiously at her but their attention remained on Carlton.

"If you have any question whatever about their intentions, detain them. Do I make myself clear?" He looked around the room at the nodding heads. "Shifts will run the same as they normally do for game weekends. Double coverage starting at midnight. Any questions?" When no one responded, Carlton gestured toward Jamison.

"This is Flagler Security Agent Jamison Krews. She's responsible for the personal safety of Shea Carter. She and her team will also be on site tomorrow starting at nine a.m. If you have any issues concerning Ms. Carter please take them directly to her. She'll have a radio and will be monitoring our frequency." He stepped aside motioning to the podium. "Jamison."

She looked around the room as she approached the podium. She needed these officers to feel the responsibility of campus safety on their shoulders as normal. She didn't want them to think they were being replaced by all the extra officers that would be in attendance.

She spoke as loud as she could, keeping her voice clear and firm, "Please don't forget that this is your turf to protect. You know how things are supposed to work. We aren't asking you to do anything different than you would during a regular game. There'll be a lot of uniforms and plainclothes officers and agents milling through the crowds. They're here to back you up and to keep issues from distracting you from your job. If someone is causing you a problem pull in an unassigned officer or agent so you can return to your specific duties. Does anyone have anything to add? Something we might have missed."

A hand rose from the back row and Jamison was thankful she remembered his name. "Yes, Jeremy."

He blushed slightly from being identified by name but stepped forward. "What about the press? Are they still going to be allowed in the same areas?"

"Good question. Chief?" Jamison stepped aside to let Carlton answer the question.

"Yes, they'll be allowed in the same areas. However, we're doing a more in-depth background check on all of them. We asked the media earlier this week to submit projected reporters' names they planned to have onsite so all of the checks will be done by tomorrow morning. The officers working the press gate will hand out new press passes to the individuals that have been cleared. Old passes will no longer work so anyone that shows up with one that has not been cleared on the new list won't get in."

"They no longer have free run," Jamison added. "They're only allowed in their designated area. If you catch them in a restricted area or trying to access a restricted area, immediately call for backup and we'll detain them. There's going to be a lot of plainclothes officers hanging around so don't be afraid to use them."

"How will we identify the plainclothes officers?" a female voice called out.

Jamison looked at Carlton.

"All law enforcement passes will have a special fluorescent yellow TU lanyard."

"And don't be afraid to make them show identification even if they have a yellow lanyard," Jamison added. "Any more questions?"

When no one stepped forward, Carlton addressed them again. "Day shift go home. Get some sleep and come back fresh. It's going to be a long day tomorrow."

Carlton joined her as the officers filed out of the building.

"I think that went well, Chief," Jamison said as they watched the last of the stragglers leave the office.

"Yes, but I'm still worried about tomorrow."

Jamison raised her eyebrows.

"My staff of sixty-five officers handles about forty thousand students and that number can double on a normal game day. This is not a normal game day. Then we add to that number with another fifty armed officers and agents."

Jamison nodded. "I see what you're saying but I think you need to look at the upside. We have a plan and if everyone follows it we should be in good shape. Flagler officers will mingle with fans and walk the edges of the seating area. TPD will split their time but mostly they'll remain in the areas where you already have officers. With TPD there your officers can focus on their tasks and TPD can handle any problem cases. If a Flagler officer needs backup for an arrest, they'll have to call TPD or one of your officers."

"I'll have thirty officers assigned to specific posts and the rest will be roaming too."

Jamison thought for a second. "I think I'll assign sectors so they don't all bunch up."

"There are four wings. It might be easier to assign a team to each wing and not break it down any further."

Jamison glanced at her watch. She needed to get back to Shea. "I like that idea. I'm going to need copies of the map of the stadium. Can I get them now?"

"Sure." Carlton led the way back into his office and pulled open a filing cabinet drawer. "We keep these on hand year round for contractors." He handed her a stack.

"Great. I'll see you tomorrow morning."

CHAPTER NINETEEN

Jamison jogged back across campus watching the crowds of people milling around. She could see that a lot happened on campus the night before a big game. Along with some motor homes, there were cars parked everywhere. She was more than a little pleased to find the stadium doors secured and the halls inside empty. Coach Sutton's door stood open and she slowed her pace as she approached. His deep voice came through the opening but Jamison couldn't identify any specific words. She paused in the doorway when she saw Shea, alone on the couch, with her head in her hands.

Coach Sutton met her eyes and motioned her inside. "Come in, Jamison. I was just giving Shea a pep talk."

She glanced at Shea who looked up with tears in her eyes.

"That's some pep talk, Coach," Jamison said hesitantly.

Shea smiled up at her. "Coach has a way with words." She stood and joined Jamison at the door.

"Ready?" Jamison asked. Shea nodded. She wasn't sure what she had walked in on but she knew how important Shea was to him and not only as a star quarterback. "Good luck tomorrow, Coach."

"Thank you, Jamison."

As they stepped out of his office, she noticed Shea's unaccustomed empty hands. "Do you need anything before we head home?"

"Nope. I'm ready to reduce myself to a vegetative state."

Jamison smiled. Shea deserved a long break and she would get one after football season. They walked to her truck with little conversation and were headed toward her apartment when she finally asked. "Do you want to talk about why you were upset when I walked in back there?"

Shea shrugged. "Coach was just reminding me how far I've come since he met me." She paused before continuing. "And that the outcome of tomorrow's game doesn't matter," she said with a slight quiver in her voice.

She didn't need Shea to elaborate any further on the pep talk. Clearly Coach Sutton had reminded her how proud he was of her. The impact of this possibly being Shea's final game of her college career hit Jamison. They should do something special tonight. She glanced at Shea, remembering her elevated temperature earlier. "Hey, how are you feeling?"

"I'm fine. Why?"

"I was thinking we should do something special tonight but then I remembered you were running a fever earlier."

"Oh. I told you that was only a lack of sleep. I felt better after my nap and I feel fine now." She glanced at Jamison. "I'm a little drained, though. What did you have in mind?"

"Did you eat with the team?"

"Not really. I had one slice. Too many men and too little pizza."

"Good. What's your favorite food? And don't say pizza."

Shea smiled. "Well, it is pizza but a homemade lasagna with pepperoni and lots of cheese ranks near the top too."

"Would you settle for a mediocre restaurant version? There's a little place beside the grocery store on Magnolia Street."

"I know where you mean. Can we get fried ravioli too?"

Jamison shook her head in resignation. "Pasta is good carbs for tomorrow but you can't resist adding something fried, can you? You probably will want to drink wine too?"

Shea laughed. "I better skip the wine or I might fall asleep during dinner but ask me again tomorrow night."

Jamison dialed the restaurant and placed the order. A few minutes later, she parked illegally in front of the small plaza. She hurried into the restaurant, quickly paid the tab and stepped back outside to wait for their dinner. She was surprised to see Heather's car parked behind hers. Heather was dressed in matching black cargo pants and shirt with black boots. Her blond shoulder-length hair was pulled back in a ponytail and even in the dim light from the parking lot Jamison could see the excitement in her blue eyes.

"It's illegal to park here," Heather said with a grin as she approached.

"And you needed to park illegally to tell me that." Jamison returned her smile as she watched Heather lean against the side of her truck. Shea was watching the two of them, and Jamison opened her door so Shea could be included in the conversation.

"I was headed to your place when I saw your truck."

"What's up?" Jamison asked.

"I'm meeting Sheldon in about ten minutes and we're headed to the compound."

Jamison nodded and glanced at Shea to see if she had heard.

Heather continued. "We decided not to take any backup. Too much firepower might give the wrong impression. Sheldon alerted the Atlanta FBI office in case we need them, though."

Shea leaned farther across the seat. "It's going to take more than four hours to get there. They're gonna be asleep."

"Right. We're going to do a little surveillance until everyone wakes up in the morning and then we'll ask sweetly for them to send Georgie out."

Jamison nodded. "Keep us posted, okay?"

"And be careful," Shea called.

Heather returned to her car as the server from inside the restaurant brought out Jamison's order. Jamison climbed into the truck and handed Shea the carryout bag. Shea immediately dug into the bag and found the ravioli. Pulling a piece out with her fingers, she broke it in half and blew on it until it cooled enough to eat. She stuffed half into her mouth and reached across the cab waving the other half in front of Jamison's nose as she drove. She opened her mouth and Shea slid the piece inside. She felt an immediate spark as Shea let her fingers linger on her lips. Her body went from relaxed and comfortable to on fire in less than a second.

"Wow," Shea said softly, pulling her hand away from Jamison's face. "I suddenly have a craving that food won't satisfy."

Jamison chuckled. "Me too, but I've already decided to sleep on the couch tonight."

"Who said anything about sleeping," Shea mumbled.

Jamison was surprised that Shea didn't object more to her suggested sleeping arrangements. It certainly wasn't what she wanted but she needed to do what was best for Shea. Tomorrow's game was too important and she had tampered enough with Shea's normal routine.

She parked and stepped around the truck to open Shea's door. She kept Shea close as they walked into the lobby and boarded the elevator. When they entered the apartment, Shea immediately began arranging the food. She dished pasta from the carryout containers onto plates, sharing both dinners between the two of them. Pouring salad into small bowls, she set them on the table along with dressing.

Jamison watched her move around the apartment as if she belonged. She couldn't help smiling when Shea finished and turned to find her watching.

"What?" Shea asked.

"I like that you seem at home here."

Shea shrugged. "I feel at home here." She put a finger to Jamison's chest. "But I'm going to need some clothes soon."

Jamison laughed, pulling her close. Holding Shea in her arms felt natural. Like they were made for each other. She wasn't sure how long the embrace lasted but the groan of her stomach reminded her about the food waiting on the table. She kissed

Shea lightly on the lips, savoring the taste of Shea and fried ravioli. The fire she had felt earlier raced through her again and she pushed it aside. There would be plenty of time to show Shea how she felt about her after the game.

"Let's eat before it gets cold."

She glanced at Shea several times during dinner, noting the lines were back around Shea's eyes. She hoped they were caused by tiredness and game stress rather than her situation with the militia. Though Heather and Sheldon were not far from her mind, she enjoyed the quiet time with Shea. As usual the silence was comforting so she waited until they were almost finished with their meal to lift her glass of water. "It's not wine but can I make a toast anyway?"

"Of course." Shea raised an eyebrow as she lifted her glass.

"To the Tigers and a wonderful season with an amazing quarterback."

Shea smiled. "And to winning a National Championship."

She stared into Shea's eyes, searching the depth of the darkness. "And to your future."

"To *our* future."

Jamison had never wanted anything as much as she wanted Shea at that moment. Throwing aside all of her talk about no touching and sleeping in separate rooms, she walked around the table and pulled Shea to her feet. She tucked a stray hair behind Shea's ear and played with the curls at the base of her neck. Her desire was reflected in Shea's eyes. She pulled her close and kissed her. As they deepened the kiss, Shea tried to maneuver them toward the living room but Jamison held her ground.

She wanted to give in to Shea's demands but in the back of her mind she knew it wasn't the right time. The last week had been an emotional roller coaster for both of them and tonight Shea needed to rest. As much as it pained her to, she broke the kiss and rested her forehead against Shea's shoulder. When her breathing slowly returned to normal and she could feel Shea's slowing as well, she stepped away and began clearing the table.

She could see Shea wanted to say something but instead she began helping Jamison with the dishes. Standing side by side at the sink, she bumped Shea with her hip.

"Are you upset with me?"

Shea stretched the silence until Jamison glanced at her and then she smiled. "Not at all. It's clear how you feel about me. I'm touched that you care so much about me getting enough rest."

Jamison dried the last plate and placed it back in the cabinet, turning to lean on the counter. "Once all of this is over we can explore us." She grimaced. "I guess it's a little late to say that after last night but you know what I mean, right?"

"You're concerned I have Stockholm syndrome."

Jamison laughed. "I haven't exactly held you captive."

"So you say." Shea laughed and walked toward the living room.

"Should we go to bed?" Jamison asked as she followed her.

Shea pushed her onto the couch and lay down on top of her. "I thought you'd never ask."

Jamison pulled the remote from under her body and flipped on the television. "Game footage it is, then."

Shea laughed and rolled over, snuggling her back into Jamison. She finally gave up the remote as Shea guided them through each play, stopping, starting and rewinding.

Jamison's phone vibrated in her pocket. "Shit," she said. "I totally forgot about your sister." She quickly disengaged from Shea and moved into the kitchen.

"James," Mel said, "how's my little sister?"

"I can guess by your tone that you know what happened last night?"

"I just got off the phone with Mrs. Bowden and she mentioned there were some developments."

"I'm really sorry I didn't call you, Mel. It all happened so fast and by this morning TPD had screwed up and released him. What would have been good news didn't sound so good anymore."

"I get it, James. I'm just happy Shea's okay."

"Oh, she's okay." Jamison glanced up to see Shea watching her with a huge grin on her face. "FBI and TPD are on their way to Atlanta to pick McGomery up again. Hopefully by the time the game starts tomorrow he'll be back in custody."

"Are you going with the assumption he's working alone?" Mel asked.

Jamison hesitated. "I don't think he is but security is going to be out in force at the game tomorrow. I'll be by Shea's side the entire time."

"I know you got it covered. Nikki and I are still hoping to make the game. We should be leaving here within the next couple of hours."

"Your mission is complete?"

"Well...Nikki eliminated the problem so we'd just be hanging around to see the aftermath and another team can do that for us. Besides, I want to see my sister play."

"Okay. Come find us when you arrive."

"Oh, and Mom's arriving tomorrow around noon. I don't expect she'll attempt to make contact with Shea until after the game though. I didn't tell her anything. Sometimes she's better off not knowing. We usually have brunch at my place on Sunday. You should plan on being there."

Jamison wasn't sure it was an invitation. It sounded more like a demand but she didn't hesitate in her response. "I'll be there."

"Shea can give you directions. I moved last month so it's a new place."

"Okay. I'll see you Sunday if not before. Have a safe trip."

Jamison leaned against the counter, looking at Shea, who sat grinning evilly.

"My sister makes you nervous now." Shea laughed.

"Not nervous, really." Jamison hesitated. "Well, okay. It does make me a little nervous to tell her I want to date her sister."

"Date? You want to date me?"

"I want to get to know you better and to spend time with you when you're *not* being forced to endure my company."

"Yeah." Shea sighed. "It's been pretty miserable."

Jamison grimaced and pulled Shea to her feet. "Bed," she said, pushing her in the direction of the bedroom.

Shea went willingly and Jamison reclined on the small bed, giving her privacy in the bathroom. Shea emerged from the bathroom naked and crossed to the bed. Jamison pulled back the covers and was relieved when Shea crawled under willingly.

Shea pulled Jamison's arm around her body and snuggled into her. "Stay with me for a while, please," she asked softly.

Jamison knew she wouldn't refuse and shifted to find a more comfortable position, remaining on top of the comforter. Shea placed Jamison's palm over her breast before sliding it down her body and back up again. When Shea moaned, Jamison knew she was in trouble.

"Shea."

"Yeah, yeah. I know. We're sleeping."

Jamison laughed softly as Shea shifted Jamison's hand over her breast again. As much as she knew she should decline, Jamison also knew she would not. She allowed Shea to guide her fingers across each nipple, gently stroking and teasing until Shea tried to turn in her arms.

"No," Jamison said. "Relax. You're not going all crazy on me again tonight."

"But I wanna be on top," Shea whimpered.

Jamison laughed again. "I know you do but tonight you're going to relax while I coax you gently into submission."

Shea groaned. "I want hard and fast."

"But you're going to get soft and slow," Jamison said the words softly into Shea's ear as she moved her lips to Shea's neck.

True to her word, Jamison's movements remained slow until Shea's body finally gave in to her pace, cresting and falling with each touch. She held her tight each time Shea's body succumbed, wanting to continue until Shea was satisfied but relieved when her body finally relaxed against Jamison's chest. She stilled her hand, holding it tight against Shea's center.

* * *

Two hours later, Jamison's phone vibrated on the nightstand. She gently removed her hands from Shea's body and picked up the phone. Sliding out of bed, she connected the call.

"We got a problem." Todd's voice came through loud in Jamison's ear so she continued to the living room.

"What's wrong?"

"McGomery's phone just came back on and he's moving south on Interstate Seventy-Five."

"Back toward Tallahassee," she groaned. She quickly rattled off Heather's number and disconnected from Todd, telling him to call Heather in five minutes. She dialed Heather and was relieved when she picked up on the first ring.

"Heather, McGomery's phone is headed back south."

"Well shit," Heather said, relaying the information to Sheldon. "We're only about thirty minutes away from the compound."

"There are cameras on Seventy-Five and Todd is tapping into them. He can tell you exactly where the car is and maybe who's in it. I gave him your number and he'll be calling you in about five minutes."

Heather again relayed the information to Sheldon. Jamison could hear Sheldon's voice in the background as they discussed a new game plan and then Heather came back on the line. "Okay. We're going to stop here until we hear from Todd. If we can confirm McGomery's in the car we'll tail them. If not, we'll go on to the compound."

"Call me back after you make a decision. I'll be up for a while."

"Okay. Gotta run. Todd's calling." Heather disconnected.

Jamison tossed her phone on the coffee table and dropped onto the couch. She looked up seeing Shea's reflection in the television as she stood in the doorway to the bedroom. She wore Jamison's T-shirt and her hair was disheveled. She moved around the end of the couch and sat beside Jamison.

"McGomery is coming back to Tallahassee?"

Jamison pulled her into her arms. "We don't know what his plan is but Heather and Sheldon are going to stay with him." She kissed the top of Shea's head. "And he might not be in the car. Let's wait and see."

She stood and pulled Shea to her feet. "Back to bed."

Taking Shea's hand, she led her into the bedroom and held up the covers, wrapping them around Shea when she climbed in. Jamison lay next to her rubbing her back until Shea's breathing slowed. She quietly shut the bedroom door and moved into the living room. Within thirty minutes, Heather called back.

"It's McGomery and we're on him. If he stays at this pace with no stops we should be back in Tallahassee by five. He's got someone with him. Todd's running facial rec to get us a name."

"What's the plan for picking him up?"

Heather hesitated. "Sheldon wants to tail him and see where he goes first. I'll let you know when he is in custody. Otherwise you'll know we're still tailing him."

"Don't let him in the stadium."

"We won't." Heather disconnected.

Jamison rested her head against the back of the sofa and closed her eyes. After a few minutes she lay down, stretching her legs the length of the couch.

CHAPTER TWENTY

Sleep had been slow in coming but eventually it had. Now Jamison's eyes opened to sunlight streaming through her living room window. She glanced at the clock on the wall. Relieved it was only a few minutes after seven, she was surprised to have heard nothing from Sheldon and Heather. She showered quietly and then woke Shea.

She forced herself to remain standing and not join Shea in the bed. When Shea finally opened her eyes enough to convince Jamison she was awake, Jamison left her to make breakfast. She was placing two plates with a spinach and cheese omelet on the table when Shea emerged from the bedroom.

"I'm starving." Shea sat down at the table across from Jamison and quickly ate several bites. "I could get used to the good food you make, you know?"

Jamison smiled as Shea continued to inhale the eggs. She was relieved that there was no sign of the lines that had marked Shea's face the previous night. Her eyes were alive with anticipation and she looked refreshed and alert. The flirty, teasing tone that Jamison loved was back in her voice and it seemed Shea had gotten enough sleep after all.

"Normally I eat cold pizza for breakfast," Shea continued.

Jamison couldn't stop her grimace and Shea laughed. "It's good."

"What time do you need to be at the field?"

"Usually I arrive about nine-ish." Shea hesitated. "Do you have a meeting? I could go with you."

"I'm meeting with the team from Flagler at nine. I don't want to disrupt your schedule, but if you're okay with hanging with me, then so am I." She'd heard the hesitation in Shea's voice and she didn't mind if Shea attended the meeting with her. It might be good for Shea to understand that she was going to be protected and could concentrate freely on the game.

* * *

They arrived at the field ten minutes before the scheduled meeting. Jamison dropped the tailgate on the rear of her truck and she and Shea sat on it. She introduced Shea as Flagler agents began to arrive. There were a few TU officers as well and they hung near Shea, joking and talking about the game. Jamison was pleased to see Jeremy's familiar face in the group.

When Jamison had checked everyone in, she handed out maps of the stadium and assigned everyone to a group, then each group to a wing and gave them a short briefing. Leaving the agents to work out the specifics of their assignments, she turned to Jeremy.

"Jeremy, where are you assigned today?" Jamison asked, pulling the young man's attention away from Shea.

"I'm a rover, ma'am."

"Great. I want you to hang near me and Shea." She handed him an earwig and microphone connecting him to the Flagler agents.

Jamison inserted her own earwig and attached her microphone to the collar of her T-shirt. Out of habit she shifted the pistol strapped under her arm and touched each of the extra magazines stuck in the pockets of what had once been Shea's Windbreaker. Shea had laid no claim over it when it appeared at Jamison's apartment and she seemed a little pleased to see her wearing it again.

Jamison smiled at the pride on Jeremy's face to be included as Shea mumbled about wanting an earpiece too. Turning to the group, she asked if there were any questions and quickly answered the few that were asked.

"Jeremy, check in with Chief Hammer and then meet us at the locker room."

"See you in about ten," he said as he hurried off.

She looked at Shea. "Ready?"

Shea nodded.

"How's your day going to run?" Jamison asked as they walked toward the stadium entrance.

"Well, let's see. The game starts at two so I'll chill for about an hour and then I'll dress for the game. Coach Sutton will give us his standard pep talk and then we'll run through some plays on the field. I'll return to the locker room and resume my vegetative state until about forty minutes before game time when I'll return to hear more key words from Coach Sutton. Then we'll take the field for the game."

Jamison rolled her eyes at Shea's overly dramatic reciting of what her day would be like. She had never seen Shea this hyper but couldn't even begin to imagine the amount of energy Shea would need to get through this day. Jamison gave her waist a squeeze, quickly dropping her arm as they entered the coolness of the stadium. She was pleased to see the TU officers stationed at every entrance, and she and Shea showed their passes to gain access. As they climbed the stairs leading to the locker rooms, Jamison watched the vendors moving around her. The number of people already within the stadium was surprising and Jamison took a step closer to Shea.

Running footsteps sounded behind them and Jamison automatically pulled her pistol, pushing Shea behind her as she turned. She quickly took in the blue jeans, the Tigers University T-shirt and the youthful face. The approaching teenager slid to a stop several feet away from them.

Shea placed her hand on Jamison's arm and stepped around her, addressing the boy. "What is it, Andy?"

Jamison lowered her weapon but didn't return it to her holster. Her pulse was racing but she attempted to give Andy a small smile to put him at ease.

"Lyn...Lyn...Lynnette wanted me to tell you she'll meet you in the locker room in about an hour," he stuttered, never moving his eyes from Jamison's pistol. He backed away from them.

"That's fine, Andy. Thanks." Shea frowned at Jamison. "He's one of the student trainers. You can put that away."

Jamison made a full circle check and then she secured her pistol. She knew Shea was unhappy with her approach but she wasn't willing to negotiate on her safety. They walked the rest of the way to the locker room in silence.

Jamison cleared the locker room, making Shea wait inside the door until she finished. Shea had barely opened her locker when there was a knock on the door. Immediately Jamison pulled her weapon and moved toward the door shielding Shea with her body.

"Agent Krews?" Jeremy's voice sounded through the locker room door.

Jamison pulled open the door and checked the hall before addressing him. "Everything okay?"

"Yes, ma'am. Coach Sutton asked me to get Shea. He wants to walk through a couple of plays with her."

Jamison felt Shea approaching as Jeremy talked and she turned to meet her eyes. "You're on, superstar."

Shea gave her a wicked grin as she turned to follow Jeremy. They passed through the men's locker room and Shea greeted her teammates, following Jeremy through the tunnel and onto the field. Coach Sutton waited, clipboard in hand, with several other players seated on a bench. The other players, like Shea, were still dressed in shorts and T-shirts, not yet having dressed for the game.

Jamison scanned the stadium as Coach Sutton took a knee in front of the players. She only half listened as he sketched plays on his clipboard and then sent them onto the field to execute each one. She watched several TU officers sweep systematically through the stadium, catching sight of Carlton midway up the bleachers talking with two young women vendors. Jamison gestured to Carlton, letting Jeremy know she was leaving the field temporarily. She climbed the steps quickly, not sure how long the coach would keep Shea on the field.

"Carlton." Jamison stepped forward, interrupting his conversation with the two women. "Can I have a minute?"

Carlton gave her a nod and made quick introductions between her and the two young women before moving a few steps away from them.

"I'm glad you tracked me down." He handed her a radio along with an earpiece to attach to it.

"Thanks." She slid the earpiece into her pocket and clipped the radio to her belt. "You're sure it's okay if I keep Jeremy close today? I could use a second pair of eyes and he has a good relationship with Ms. Carter."

"No problem."

"How'd the sweep of the stadium go this morning?"

"All clear. Did they pick McGomery up last night?"

Jamison frowned. "He changed direction a little after midnight, coming back toward Tallahassee. He's being followed to get as much information as they can before grabbing him."

Jamison noticed Shea and her teammates exiting the field so she gave Carlton a wave and ran down the steps to join them.

"Looks like you're stuck with us today. You good with that?" Jamison asked Jeremy.

"Yes, ma'am."

"Okay, then cut the ma'am crap. Jamison will do."

He gave her a shy smile. Somehow she got the feeling he might not be able to censor his politeness that easily but she smiled back at him. Falling into step with Shea, the three entered the tunnel and passed through the men's locker room. Jamison studied the short hallway in both directions as they took the few steps across the hall to enter the women's locker room. She was surprised but pleased to see the reporters weren't camped out yet and that ropes had been placed to block their access.

Jamison quickly cleared the locker room again as Shea pulled a mat from the stack and pulled it close to her locker. She lay down on it with her feet on the nearby bench. Headphones in her ears and her eyes closed, she tapped her feet to the beat of the music. Jamison took a seat on the stacked mats in the corner and studied the stadium diagram. She memorized the entrances and the location of each of her team leaders. The radio on her hip suddenly crackled as TU officers rushed to assist TPD officers with a fight outside the stadium. Carlton's voice came through the speaker as he quickly checked in with each of his supervisors. Jamison pulled the earpiece from her pocket but before she could attach it to the radio, blocking the exterior speaker, Carlton spoke to Jeremy.

"Unit four two, is the cub secure?"

"Affirmative."

Jamison adjusted the volume in her ear and glanced up to see Shea's eyes filled with laughter.

"Did he…did he really just call me the 'cub'?"

Jamison considered playing dumb but she knew Shea would see right through her so she only smiled. "You should be happy. It could've been kitten."

Shea grasped a nearby towel and threw it at Jamison.

The locker room door opened and Jeremy announced Lynnette. Jamison rested her hand on her weapon until the door was shut again. With a nod at Lynnette, she sat down on the mats and resumed her study of the stadium.

She tried not to watch as Lynnette ran her hands over Shea's legs and ribs, checking previous injuries. There was nothing sexual about it but to Jamison's surprise she still felt a twinge of jealousy. As if sensing Jamison's discomfort, Shea gave her a reassuring smile.

Lynnette finished and stepped back, raising her hands in surrender, looking back and forth between them. "What's going on with you two? Is there an injury I need to know about?" Her gaze zeroed in on Shea.

Shea laughed. "No, I'm fine. You walked in on a conversation we hadn't finished yet."

Lynnette raised her eyebrows.

"Wait a minute." Shea narrowed her eyes at Lynnette. "Did you know Hammer was calling me cub?"

Lynnette's laughter exploded and it took her some moments to regain her composure. "I didn't know before this morning." Seeing the look on Shea's face she shook her head and said vehemently, "I swear I didn't."

"Well, she did."

Jamison could see Shea nod in her direction but kept her focus on the map in her hands.

"Talk to Carlton," Jamison said under her breath.

"Oh, I plan to." Shea smiled despite the tone of voice. "And neither of you should warn him that I know." She swung her legs onto the table and Lynnette began wrapping an ankle.

Finally Lynnette finished and gave Shea a pat on her leg. "Good luck." She gathered her supplies and Jamison pulled the door open for her.

Jamison glanced up and down the hall, seeing that the media had arrived and were eager for a glimpse of Shea.

"Everything okay out here?" she asked Jeremy.

"Yes, ma'am…I mean Jamison."

She smiled at him and ducked back inside. Shea, wearing only a black sports bra, had pulled on her padded spandex shorts and was bent over stepping into her shiny black game pants. Jamison leaned against the wall watching as the softness she had felt hours ago transformed into the hard lines of a game-driven veteran. Her back to Jamison, she lifted each foot onto the bench and tied her cleats. Sitting on the floor with her shoulder pads between her legs, Shea pulled her black and teal game jersey over the hard plastic. Then she pushed the shoulder pads aside and lay back again with her feet and legs elevated on the bench.

Time passed quickly as Jamison stared at the game jersey with *Carter* stenciled across the back. How many times had she watched this woman on television as she led her team up and down the field? And now here she sat. Jamison swallowed the lump forming in her throat as the magnitude of the day overtook her. She watched Shea's relaxed breathing and allowed the rhythm to steady her too. Shea was prepared for today and Jamison knew it was up to her to make sure nothing off the field influenced Shea's performance.

A knock at the door brought Jamison to her feet.

"It's time," Jeremy said.

"I'll be right out, Jeremy. Just give me a minute," Shea said in a voice Jamison wasn't sure she recognized.

Shea pulled a gel pack from her locker and squeezed the contents into her mouth. Jamison watched her as she lifted the shoulder pads above her head and slid them on. She shifted around pulling her rib protector into place, glancing up at Jamison with an evil grin.

"Think you can stop drooling long enough to help me?"

Jamison couldn't help smiling back. "Maybe." She stepped closer to her. "How can I help?"

Shea lifted up her jersey and showed Jamison how to secure the pads. Shea grasped the neck of the pads and pulled down, holding it in position. "Tighten it now." She held her breath until all the straps were secured. Breathing deeply, she picked up her helmet and headed for the door.

Jamison was captivated by her appearance. With her height, Shea was already an imposing figure but now she looked like a warrior heading into battle. Jamison shook her head to clear the fog of the beauty in front of her.

"Shea, wait."

Shea turned and smiled at her. "I gotta go." She tapped her wrist where a watch would be. "Team meeting."

"Right." Jamison nodded. "Just let me check the hallway first."

She stepped in front of Shea and pulled open the door. Softly over her shoulder she said, "You really are breathtaking."

She heard Shea's laugh as they entered the hall. Jeremy jumped ahead of them and held the door open. Flashbulbs exploded and voices hurled questions at Shea as they took the couple of steps to reach the men's locker room. Jamison stepped aside, letting Shea enter first and then followed her inside quickly closing the door on the noise.

She looked at Jeremy. "Is it always like this?"

Jeremy beamed with pride. "Pretty much. Like you said earlier…" He motioned at Shea as she joined her teammates seated around the whiteboard. "Superstar."

Coach Sutton only had a few words of encouragement for them and then they all stood, bowing their heads. Jamison watched as each player reached out to touch another player or coach. When they were all connected, she heard a soft voice from inside the huddle begin to pray. As a child she had been forced to attend church each Sunday and it was a chore she always wanted to escape. This prayer was nothing like Jamison had ever experienced. A feeling of peace quickly engulfed her as she felt Jeremy's hand touch her shoulder, connecting her to the team. Jamison bowed her head and said her own silent prayer that everyone in attendance today, players and fans, would all be safe from harm.

Jamison lifted her head and met Shea's eyes. She crossed the room in two strides with Jeremy at her heels as they joined Shea for the walk through the tunnel. Though they had done this every day for the last week, today felt different. The electricity coursing through the players was different too. There was still joking and some pushing and shoving but there was a seriousness to them all as well. At the edge of the tunnel, the players in front stopped and waited for Shea to join them. She pulled her helmet over her head and her teammates followed her as they jogged onto the field.

Jamison rubbed the goose bumps on her arms as she listened to the roar of the crowd. She watched Shea stop in the middle of the field and be engulfed by her team. Jamison could see her leaning in to whisper to each player as she passed back through them before they separated into lines to begin their warm-up exercises.

She followed Jeremy as they joined the coaches and athletic trainers on the sidelines. The roar of the crowd was so loud Jamison could no longer distinguish the voices in her earpieces. She stepped closer to Jeremy as she pulled out the earpiece connected to the TU radio and let it dangle across her shoulder.

"Remove the earpiece I gave you, Jeremy. Focus only on TU security." She motioned to her dangling cord. "I've got Flagler. Let me know if there's anything going on."

Jeremy did as she asked. They stood silently watching the pregame festivities, their attention focused on scanning the area around the field that could pose an immediate threat to Shea's safety. The crowd was loud and boisterous. Jamison did her best to blend in with the activity on the sidelines though she did unzip her Windbreaker for better access to her pistol.

CHAPTER TWENTY-ONE

Shea's concentration was completely focused on the game. The threat to her own safety was at the back of her mind now as she walked onto the field for the traditional coin toss. She always picked heads. Her logic was sound as heads was always on top. When the coin fell the Tigers' way, Shea quickly motioned they would kick off now and receive in the second half.

As she left the field to the roar of the crowd, she quickly located Jamison on the sideline. She wished she could go to her or even stand near her, but she needed to be ready when the ball was put in her hands. She stopped at the line of coaches and they immediately surrounded her going over the first plays she would run. The kickoff, with the wind to their backs, carried the ball through the opposite end zone for a touchback.

Shea watched the Tigers defense take the field with confidence and within minutes she was watching special teams fair catch a punt on the twenty-yard line. She jogged onto the field blocking out the roar of the crowd. Her fingers tingled with anticipation to touch the football and she pulled them into a fist and then opened them several times. Placing her hands on the shoulders of her offensive line, she stepped into the huddle and called a pass play designed to give her multiple options. She'd have three receivers down field and a running back beside her.

Shea touched Josh's back as she stepped behind him in the formation and began calling the cadence. At the impact of the ball in her hands, she spun right, faking a handoff to her running back as her eyes scanned the field. Adrenaline coursed through her and she zeroed in on Jared, a wide receiver. He had a step on his defender and any minute he would cut toward the open hole in the middle of the field. Trusting her receiver to be in the correct spot by the time the ball got there, she pulled back and threw a perfect spiral into the hole. Jared stretched his entire body pulling the ball tight against him as he turned toward the goal line. He managed to gain another ten yards before the Jacksonville defense stopped him but the Tigers were across the fifty-yard line.

Her insides screaming with celebration, she slapped Jared hard on top of his helmet as he entered the huddle. She called basically the same play again. Her receivers ran different patterns but the play allowed her to decide where to put the ball. As she dropped back from center, she could see the right side of her offensive line caving in so she swung left searching the field and pulling the defense toward her. Across the field, Andy, another wide receiver, cut back toward her a second before his defensive counterpart made the cut as well. Shea arched the ball high, clearing the bodies at midfield. She didn't like the risk of throwing across the players but Andy had made a beautiful cut and he deserved the ball. Andy made the catch at the ten-yard line as the defense slammed him hard to the ground.

Shea wanted to throw again but knew she had to put it on the ground this time. She looked at her five-foot-nine running back and smiled confidently as she called the play. She quickly passed the ball to Darren and continued her rollout as if to make another pass. She spun back toward the mass in front of her in time to see Darren cross the goal line. This time she allowed herself to celebrate. Jumping up and down, she joined her teammates in their mass exodus off the field. The extra point was good and the Tigers were up by seven.

Shea took a seat on the bench bombarded with water and towels. She pulled her helmet from her head and wiped her face. She searched the crowd around her for Jamison. A touch of panic had started to set in when she felt a soft hand on the back of her neck. She knew Jamison's touch and she let her body relax against Jamison's thighs. She knew the cameras were probably on her but she didn't care. She needed to know Jamison was close and touching her made everything right, allowing her to turn her attention back to the game.

* * *

Jamison stood behind Shea with her arms folded across her chest. She was awestruck at Shea's performance. Shea was unbelievable on the field. She had tried not to scream and act as crazy as the rest of the folks on the sideline but couldn't stop herself. The Tigers had moved the ball down the field like there wasn't another team out there. Shea had made it all look easy. She knew it wouldn't continue that way as the game progressed but she took a few minutes to bask.

The Tigers continued to roll over Jacksonville and the crowd seemed to get louder with each play both on offense and defense. Jamison's ears throbbed with the noise and she often had to press her earpiece tighter into her ear to hear conversations. According to Jeremy, TPD had made four arrests already and had another five people in custody for suspicious behavior. An FBI drug dog had hit on two people trying to enter the stadium and they were being detained and interrogated. Jamison's Flagler crew had been fairly quiet.

At halftime, Jamison gave Liam a welcoming nod as he approached and motioned for him to join them as they followed Shea and the Tigers into the tunnel. Away from the roar of the crowd, Jamison asked, "What's going on?"

"I thought maybe you could use some extra eyes today. I didn't think I'd be able to make it but I called Chief Hammer this morning and he left me a pass at the gate."

"That's great. We appreciate the help. It's been fairly quiet for us."

Shea motioned for Jamison to take the lead. "Can we go? I need to get back in here quickly."

Jamison pulled open the door and checked the hallway before leading the way across the hall and into the women's locker room. Shea danced impatiently as she waited for Jamison to quickly clear the room and allow her access. Placing her helmet on the bench, Shea disappeared into a bathroom stall. A few seconds later she came out holding her pants closed with one hand.

"Can you tie this and buckle my belt?"

Jamison laughed. "Of course. Come here." She pulled the laces tight and tied them, tucking the ends inside Shea's pants and buckling the belt. "How did you manage all season?"

"Usually Lynnette follows me. I guess she figured I wouldn't need her today." She winked at Jamison and leaned in giving her a quick kiss.

"Hey knock that off, superstar. People are waiting for you." Jamison smiled at her. "You were awesome out there. You make it look effortless."

"I wish it were that easy. The last couple of plays they were really closing in on me. I'm not sure if my line is just getting tired or if they're reading our plays."

Jamison opened the door and stepped aside, allowing Shea to follow Jeremy back to the men's locker room. She and Liam brought up the rear. They all stepped inside the chaos of the room and Shea went straight to the table filled with fresh fruit. She grabbed several pieces and then chose a chair in the front row. Jamison, Liam and Jeremy leaned against the wall and listened to Coach Sutton map out the second half of the game.

As she had been all week, Jamison was again impressed with the attitude and camaraderie of the team. There was no showboating or trash talking. Everyone was zeroed in on the fundamentals of the game and what was required of them to go on to win. Jamison watched Shea's reactions to what Coach Sutton had to say and then watched the rest of the team follow Shea's lead. The dynamics were amazing. Shea led by example on and off the field. There was a kind of bond among the team that only developed over time. She had seen military units work the same way. The strong connection holding the team together and allowing them to move as one. Each member focused on performing their portion of the task at hand.

The team stood, reaching toward the center where Shea now stood. Jamison couldn't hear what she said but her eyes moved around the group focusing on each player. Several heads nodded in agreement with what Shea was saying. Shea broke the huddle with a loud war chant that was made louder as the rest of the team joined in.

Jamison and her team followed Shea through the tunnel, hanging back a bit as Shea joked with her teammates. As the team ran through a few warm-ups for the second half, Jamison was surprised to see Heather and Sheldon standing behind the Tigers' bench. They had changed into jeans and T-shirts. Their shirts were tucked behind the badges fastened to the front of their jeans and they looked like twins. Each stood with an open stance, their arms folded across their chests. Jamison tapped Jeremy and Liam and the three headed over to them.

As Jamison approached her eyes flicked between the two trying to get a read on the situation. They both looked tired but their eyes were clear. Heather waited until they were close enough to be heard. "We picked McGomery up a little while ago. He checked out his storage unit and house before heading to the stadium."

"He didn't like the police tape we decorated with?" Jamison asked and then made introductions.

Sheldon shook her head. "He was a bit upset with it all."

"Didn't like that we had his mother in custody either," Heather added. "Which worked in our favor. We agreed to let her go if he gave us the details of what was being planned for today."

Jamison felt her pulse race. "And?"

"The militia or whoever is running this show was smart enough not to tell Georgie anything."

"And you believe him?" Liam asked.

Sheldon and Heather both nodded.

"Todd tapped into their vehicle communication system and we were able to listen to their conversation during most of the drive. They didn't know what else to do, that's why they were headed to the stadium. They gave up the name of the guy they were supposed to meet and Todd's running facial recognition on the footage recorded by stadium cameras today." Sheldon pulled up a picture on her phone and showed it to Jamison.

Liam leaned over Jamison's shoulder for a better view. "The name?" he asked.

"Robert Sullivan," Heather provided.

"Krews!" The voice came through Jamison's earpiece and she held her hand up for everyone to stop talking.

"I'm here, Tinnes."

"I might have something. I'm following a vendor wearing a backpack. He was moving at a quick pace until he saw me and then he started a duck and run. We're on level two inside Gate G." His voice grew more excited as he talked. "He just entered the bathroom."

"Hold your position, Tinnes. Wait for backup." She glanced at Liam and then to Shea. Shea had her helmet on ready to take the ball after the kickoff.

"Go." Liam had heard the conversation in his headset as well. "Go, Krews," he said again when Jamison hesitated. "Jeremy and I got her covered."

Jamison looked toward the tunnel and then up to level two. Running to the wall behind the Tigers bench, she planted her foot about halfway up and pushed, grabbing the bar blocking the fans from the field. She swung herself over the metal bars and headed toward the ramp leading into the vendor area. With the voices of the agents responding to Tinnes's call and the roar of the crowd she couldn't hear the footsteps of Heather and Sheldon but could feel their presence behind her. As they neared Gate G, Jamison slowed to a fast walk and quickly briefed them before turning her attention back to the Flagler agents.

"Tinnes, set a perimeter and push the fans back," Jamison yelled into her microphone as she ran the last several feet.

Tinnes and another agent were attempting to keep the crowd away from the bathroom entrance. Jamison quickly realized they needed a uniform and she grabbed the TU radio at her belt. "Flagler agents have cornered a suspicious individual inside the bathroom at Gate G and we need assistance for crowd control."

Immediately several voices answered and within seconds two TU officers appeared. Jamison motioned for Tinnes to lead the way into the bathroom, leaving the other Flagler agent to work the crowd. With Sheldon and Heather on her heels, Jamison saw that the urinals were not in use but both stall doors were closed. Tinnes kicked the first one open, finding it empty. Jamison leveled her pistol on the door of the second stall as Tinnes kicked it open.

"Down on the ground," Jamison commanded to the scruffy, terrified-looking young man squatting with his feet on the toilet seat.

Tinnes holstered his weapon and pulled him from the stall, pushing him to the ground. Quickly he patted him down and secured his wrists with a plastic restraint.

"He doesn't have the backpack," Tinnes said, looking at Jamison. "I'm sure he didn't pass it to anyone. There were only three men in here when he came in and I'd have noticed if they were carrying it when they came out."

"Then it has to be here," Sheldon said, looking around the small room.

"Here." Heather pulled on black leather tactical gloves and began digging through the large metal trash can under the sink. She pulled the black backpack from inside the can and set it on the floor. Gently she pulled the zipper to get a view inside. Standing, she stepped away from the bag. "We need a bomb team."

Sheldon and Jamison both spoke immediately into their microphones. The bathroom door opened before Jamison had completed her request and Kinsey walked in with Jack.

"I heard Tinnes call you and headed this way. Let me take a look. I can see what we're dealing with." She held up a hand to Jack and he immediately sat.

Jamison nodded for Tinnes to pull their captive into a sitting position and she knelt in front of him. "Why are you carrying explosives?"

He shrugged.

"Who else is working with you?"

Again he shrugged.

Kinsey stood with the explosives in hand. "We're good. He didn't activate the charge yet. See here." She held the bomb up for everyone, including the suspect, to see. "He'd have to stick this piece into the explosives and then pull this out. It separates the igniter from the explosive." As she spoke, Kinsey did each of the tasks making the bomb active.

Jamison spoke slowly, "Kinsey, what are you doing?"

Kinsey gently placed the bomb back into the backpack and stood, lifting it by the straps. She walked toward the suspect and stopped in front of him. Over his head, she gave Jamison a wink.

"I'm just helping him out."

Kinsey squatted in front of him and set the backpack in his lap. His eyes were huge and filled with panic.

"That's what you wanted, right?" Kinsey asked. "To make the bomb explode?"

His eyes grew wider and he started to squirm on the floor, trying to get the backpack off his lap.

"What's wrong, man?" Kinsey asked. "Weren't you trying to set it off?"

"I...I was just supposed to place it in a trash can at Gate G. I don't know how to turn it on or off."

Kinsey nodded. "Okay that's a start. Who was supposed to wire it?"

The man looked down at the backpack in his lap and his whole body shook. "He was Scooter's friend. He said no one was going to get hurt. The bombs would be detonated after the game if the Tigers won."

"And if they didn't win?"

"I was supposed to collect them before I left the stadium."

"Them!" Jamison stepped toward him.

The man dipped his head. "I had three backpacks. The other two are still at the vendor stand. I hadn't placed them yet."

Jamison stood and looked at Heather and Sheldon. "We need a coordinated search. He might not be the only idiot they hired."

"How do we find your friend Scooter?" Sheldon asked the suspect.

"He's selling pizza at Gate C."

"Did he bring in backpacks too?"

The man shrugged. "Probably. It was good money."

Sheldon shook her head as she turned back to Jamison. "We probably shouldn't assume they haven't been activated but I don't want to pull the dogs from the entrances."

"Have the TU officers locate the packs and I'll collect each one," Kinsey suggested.

Jamison nodded and pulled out her cell phone, dialing Carlton.

"Is the cub okay?" Carlton asked without greeting her.

Jamison's heart lurched. "She was when I left her. Jeremy's with her."

"Okay then. She's fine or he would've called me." She heard him sigh. "What's going on?"

"We found an explosive device at Gate G but it wasn't activated yet. Can you coordinate a search of the rest of the stadium? Ask your officers to call it in when they find one and Flagler Agent Brooks will collect it. The bombs might be inside generic black backpacks."

"I'm on it."

Jamison looked at Kinsey who stood beside her. "Take one of the TU officers and start with the two at the vendor booth, please."

Kinsey called Jack to her and they left the bathroom.

Jamison looked at Heather. "Can you have TPD pick up this guy and Scooter?"

Heather smiled. "Already done."

"Sounds like you guys got this so I am headed back down to the field." Jamison waited as Sheldon's phone rang.

"What do you have, Todd?" Sheldon pressed a finger to her opposite ear to block the stadium noise.

Jamison and Heather waited while Sheldon listened for several seconds and then grabbed Heather's hand, to use as a writing pad, jotting down several numbers.

With a huge smile she relayed Todd's information to Jamison and Heather. "Todd found our guy on facial recognition entering Gate B. He searched the scanned tickets through that gate at the same time and linked him to seat number one, row fifty-six in section thirty-three." She read the numbers from where she had written them on Heather's hand. "He's trying to locate the identity of seat number two as well as tracking who made the purchase of the tickets."

Heather looked at the numbers on her hand and rolled her eyes at Sheldon. "I carry a notepad, you know?"

"Yeah, me too," Sheldon answered with an evil grin. She looked at Jamison. "Let's go get this fucker."

"Hold on. Let's get surveillance on him first." Jamison pulled out her cell phone again and dialed Carlton. After getting the location of the television trailers, Jamison pocketed her phone and the three of them headed outside the stadium.

CHAPTER TWENTY-TWO

Carlton held the trailer door open and the three women followed him inside. Television monitors covered one wall. Two women sat on either side dwarfed by a large man with a huge belly. They all stared intently at the screens. One of the women held up a hand for them to wait. Jamison watched as one of the cameras panned the Tiger sideline and she caught a glimpse of Shea standing beside Liam and Jeremy. Shea wore a huge smile on her face as she removed her helmet and laughed at something Liam said to her. Her sweat-soaked hair was plastered to her head and she swiped a hand through it pushing it out of her eyes.

Heather read the numbers from her hand and Carlton directed the cameraman to the proper section. They all stared silently as the man in question dipped his hand into a bag of popcorn on his lap. He chewed slowly, his attention never straying from the game. He sat on the aisle with the two seats to his left empty. He didn't seem to be talking with anyone in front of or behind him.

"Now can we go get the fucker?" Sheldon asked.

Jamison nodded. "Carlton can you stay here and let us know if he moves or if anyone joins him?"

"Absolutely."

The three women left the trailer with Jamison issuing instructions as they ran back toward the stadium. "Heather, get some uniformed officers to come down from the top of the stadium behind him."

Heather was already dialing as Jamison talked.

"Do we have a warrant for Sullivan?"

"We do," Heather answered.

They showed their passes and entered the stadium. Jamison oriented herself to the stadium map in her head. A few people still milled around in the concourse area but most had returned to their seats. Jamison took off at a jog to the right. At the first tunnel leading to the seating section she stopped. "Heather, go up about midway before heading over and we'll come in from the other side."

Heather pulled her shirt over her badge and began walking down the tunnel.

Jamison and Sheldon jogged to the next entrance and then slowed to a walk. Sheldon had already covered her badge and Jamison zipped her Windbreaker halfway to do the same. They stepped out of the tunnel into the roar of the crowd. Jamison leaned against the metal handrail and glanced around. "There's no way to approach without him seeing us."

Sheldon winked at her. "Follow my lead." She started up the stairs, reaching behind her to take Jamison's hand. She said in a falsetto, "Come on, honey. Let's find our seats."

Jamison cringed but followed her. Stopping or resisting would only draw more attention to them now. At the first landing, Jamison drew even with Sheldon, her body pressed against Sheldon's back. "I'm going to kill you, you know?"

Sheldon threw her head back and laughed as if Jamison had said something really funny. She stepped around a fan, gripping Jamison's hand tighter as they passed Sullivan.

Sheldon spun, dropping Jamison's hand and squatted behind Sullivan. She grasped his arms and pulled them tight against his sides. The bag of popcorn flew into the aisle and rolled down several stairs. Jamison couldn't hear Sheldon's whisper but she could tell by the look on Sullivan's face that he didn't like what she was saying.

Sheldon raised her voice as she stood, pulling Sullivan to his feet. "Robert Sullivan, you're under arrest."

Heather slid between Sheldon and Jamison with a pair of handcuffs which she slapped none too gently on his wrists. Heather and the TPD officers led him down the steps to the tunnel exit.

A sudden roar of anger from the crowd caught Jamison's attention and her heart stopped when she saw Shea lying on the field. Lynnette and several others from the Tigers sideline sprinted onto the field and she held her breath until they helped Shea to her feet. Sheldon nudged her as they watched the replay on the jumbo screen. Shea released the ball on a pass play, and was slammed to the ground by a defender. When he was too slow getting off their quarterback several offensive lineman tossed him aside, clearing the path for the Tigers's medics.

"She's pretty tough," Sheldon stated as the jumbo screen switched to Shea pacing the sidelines. Her helmet was still on her head even though the rules required her to sit out at least one play.

"Yes, she is." Jamison watched the screen, searching for any sign that she was injured.

"Still want to jump in there and kick some ass though, don't you?"

"Yeah but she'd probably beat me to it," Jamison said more to herself than to Sheldon. She knew her words were true but she still wanted to keep Shea safe. She realized Sheldon was now watching her instead of the jumbo screen and she tilted her head toward the field. "I think I'll head down there now."

"Okay. Don't hurt anyone. I'll let you know when Sullivan starts singing." Sheldon smiled and touched her arm as they reached the tunnel. "I'll call you myself."

Jamison made her way back down to the field. If it wasn't for drawing attention she would have jumped the railing. As tough as Shea was she had been hit hard and she needed to make sure she was okay. She hoped, and not for the first time in the last forty-eight hours, that they had finally stopped the threat against Shea and the Tigers.

Shea was sitting on the bench with her helmet off. She looked angry. Jamison stepped behind her where Liam had been standing and gently touched her neck.

Shea immediately turned with a look of relief on her face. "Are you okay?"

Jamison chuckled. "I was going to ask you the same thing. That was quite a hit."

"It was nothing but Coach is using it as an excuse to keep me on the sidelines."

Jamison glanced at Liam and he shrugged. "Medic says she might have a concussion and everyone thinks they have enough of a lead to let her sit for a while. Maybe for the rest of the game."

Jamison grimaced. She knew Shea wanted to be on the field. She glanced at the scoreboard and her face spread into a smile. The Tigers were on top thirty-four to seven with only four minutes left in the game. Jamison put a hand on Shea's arm and directed her back to the bench. "Have a seat, superstar. I think your day is over."

Shea rolled her eyes but obeyed. When the second string quarterback was taken down for a loss, Shea was back on her feet. She joined the coaches as they all talked animatedly, waving their arms and pointing at the field. Jamison was pleased to see that Shea had left her helmet on the bench and wasn't trying to get back in the game. She seemed content for the moment to assist from the sideline.

With all the timeouts, the final four minutes on the clock lasted over ten minutes even though the Tigers offense stayed with running plays to keep it moving. Jamison, Liam and Jeremy rushed to Shea's side as the final seconds ticked off and the Tigers sideline erupted in celebration. The cameras swooped in immediately and the coaches took their time herding the players toward the locker room. Jamison allowed Shea room to move but stayed close. Shea accepted congratulations from the Jacksonville players and was interviewed by several networks before Coach Sutton finally rescued her and they headed for the locker room.

As they stepped into the tunnel the noise from the celebrating crowd dropped to a low rumble and Jeremy finally relaxed the finger he had pressed to his headset.

"Everything okay, Jeremy?" Jamison asked, watching his face as they walked.

He nodded. "Just the postgame traffic."

"Go help out. We're good here."

"If you're sure. It's a mess out there."

"Go. Get it cleared so we can get out of here too." Jamison handed him the radio Carlton had given her earlier. "Return this to the chief for me, okay?"

As Jeremy made his way through the locker room, Jamison removed her earpiece connecting her to the other Flagler agents and slid it into her pocket. She leaned against the wall beside Liam, her attention on Shea again. She was talking to yet another reporter on the far side of the room and the distance between them made her uneasy.

Coach Sutton stepped out of his office and stopped beside Jamison.

"Congratulations Coach," Jamison and Liam said together.

"Thank you." He shook both of their hands. "We've got a couple of hard weeks ahead of us before the championship game." He stared at the players running around the room. "Where are we with this situation?" He motioned toward Shea.

"TPD grabbed McGomery this morning and he led us to another guy who's in custody now." Jamison didn't see a need to tell him about the bombs they had gathered during the game since none were active and Kinsey had given the all clear. Carlton would fill him in later.

"And that's it?"

Jamison grimaced. "I'd like to have the person that started it all before we call it quits."

"That's what I wanted to hear." He patted her arm. "It's time to end this party." Walking into the center of the room, he greeted the media and congratulated players and coaches. Then, holding his hands up until the room finally quieted he declared, "It's been a good season and thanks to the win today we aren't finished yet." The room erupted in cheering and he held his hands up for silence again. "We have two weeks to prepare for Atlanta and I don't want to waste a minute. Go home tonight and celebrate safely, take tomorrow off and be ready to hit it hard on Monday. Athletic trainers will be around the weight room tomorrow if anyone needs to come in for therapy, or call the office to set something up." Before the noise increased again he called, "It's time for the press to go." He looked at his assistant coaches and they began moving around the room, herding reporters toward the door. When they reached the reporter with Shea, he shook her hand and headed for the door.

Shea spoke to a few more teammates and then headed for Jamison, pulling off her shoulder pads to expose a black and teal T-shirt soaked with sweat.

"I need a shower!"

"I'm expecting press in the hallway since they were just kicked out of here so let's move fast."

Liam took the lead. They moved together into the hallway and Liam pushed through the crowd clearing a path. Shea ignored the reporters, giving them only a wave. When they stepped inside the women's locker room, Shea took up her normal position inside the door while Jamison and Liam cleared the room.

Liam touched his earpiece. "The Flagler crew is meeting in the parking lot right now to debrief. I'm heading out there before they disperse. I'll be back to help you get the superstar to your car."

"Sounds good. Call me on your way back. I'm keeping the door locked."

She crossed the room, stopping at the entrance to the shower and watched Shea under the spray, arms stretched above her head, her body glistened under the dim lights. The water dripping off her body held Jamison's gaze.

Shea stepped toward her, wrapping a towel around her shoulders. "Let's take those thoughts in your head and go home."

Jamison could only nod. Her voice lost in her desire to be with Shea.

Shea stopped in front of her and leaned in for a kiss, brushing her cool lips across Jamison's.

"Get dressed or we're not going to make it home," Jamison groaned.

Shea laughed and stepped away from her.

Jamison took her usual seat on the mats against the wall and tried to think about the best way to exit the stadium. Shea's naked body kept intruding and she rubbed her face to clear the image. Her phone vibrated in her pocket. Sheldon's number displayed. Instantly on alert, hearing sirens in the background, Jamison skipped the greetings. "What's going on?"

"Jamison, where are you?"

"We're in the women's locker room."

"Get out! Now!"

"What the hell is going on?" Jamison stood, motioning for Shea to dress quickly.

"Sullivan claims there's a bomb close enough to the locker room to take Shea out." Jamison could hear her cursing at someone in the background. "We're on our way, if Heather doesn't crash us first." Sheldon cursed again and Jamison could hear Heather's not so pleasant response in the background.

Sheldon's voice dropped an octave lower. "We're pretty confident he's lying and it's only an attempt to flush you out, so watch your ass."

Shit! Jamison unlocked the door and glanced into the empty hallway. "How close are you guys? I'm alone here."

"Five minutes tops. Just get out of there now."

She knew Shea wouldn't follow her without an explanation but she didn't want her to panic. "We need to get out of the stadium quickly. Any suggestions on the best route?"

Shea picked up her full duffel bag from the bench beside her.

"Leave it," Jamison said firmly.

"No. If we're headed back to your house then I need the clothes."

"I'll take you by your place. Please leave the bag."

"Tonight?"

Jamison had enough of the conversation. "Shea, leave the bag and come with me now."

Shea must have seen something in Jamison's face or heard enough in her voice because she dropped the bag and pushed Jamison toward the door. "Go right and we can follow the vendors' tunnel. It'll take us longer to get back to the truck but the majority of it will be outside the stadium."

At the door, Jamison pulled her pistol, holding it down beside her leg. She didn't want to scare anyone but Sheldon had been vague enough on her details that she didn't want to be empty-handed. She grasped Shea's hand and pulled her tight against her back. "Watch behind us, Shea, and if you see anyone tell me. Anyone at all. Even someone you know."

Jamison's phone vibrated but she didn't want to free up either hand to answer it. "Can you reach my phone?"

Shea slid her hand into Jamison's pocket and retrieved the phone. "It's Sheldon." Her voice held a slight tremble and Jamison squeezed her hand tighter.

"Answer it."

"Sheldon? It's Shea...she's right here. We're headed toward the vendors' tunnel. It's the fastest way out of the stadium... Okay."

"What did she say?" Jamison asked as Shea slid the phone back into her pocket.

"Keep moving. They're here and will find us."

They entered an open concourse and Jamison hesitated. Speed dictated a move straight across the opening but being in the open went against her training. She pulled Shea closer to the wall but stayed far enough away to give herself reaction time if one of the doors opened. Trying to move as fast as they could safely, Jamison felt the air ripple past her head before she heard the echo of the gunshot. She pushed Shea to the floor behind a concrete pillar.

"Was...was that a shot?" Shea asked.

Jamison nodded. "Stay down, okay?" She was trying to figure out where the shot had come from.

Another shot pinged off the concrete pillar and Jamison saw movement in the shadows under the stairs across the concourse. She wanted to fire back but couldn't be sure it was the location of the gunman. The echo of each shot ricocheted around the concourse making it impossible to pinpoint a location. She concentrated her focus on the darkness under the stairs and stuck her head out, ducking back in quickly as the ping echoed off the pillar again. This time she saw the muzzle flash in the shadow and she squeezed off two rapid shots. She heard pounding footsteps approaching from the vendor tunnel and moved her body to shield Shea.

"Jamison!" Jeremy yelled as he came into sight.

"Get down," Shea screamed at him.

Jeremy dropped as he slid behind the pillar, crashing into Shea. "I heard...I came...are you okay?" he asked, breathlessly.

Jamison wasted no time in using him. Her first priority was getting Shea to safety. She pointed at a blue door closest to their position. "Is that room unlocked?"

"I have a key," Jeremy panted.

"Go open it and clear the room. We need to get Shea out of the open."

Jeremy began crawling toward the door and Jamison unloaded her clip into the shadows under the stairs. She quickly popped in a new clip as Jeremy called out the room was clear.

"Go, Shea." Jamison could feel her hesitate. "Go, Shea and close the door behind you. Do not open it for anyone but me. Okay?"

"Okay."

Jamison focused on the shadows again and began firing as she felt Shea leave the cover of the pillar. When the door clicked shut behind Shea, Jamison stopped firing. The concourse was silent, though Jamison's ears still rang from the gunshots. The shadows under the stairs were eerily quiet and Jamison wanted to move closer but knew she needed to wait for backup. She pressed her Flagler microphone. "Liam?" she said softly.

"James? Where are you?"

"Mel?"

"Yes. Where are you?"

"In the first concourse outside the women's locker room. I have at least one gunman pinned down. Where are you?"

"Nikki and I are entering the stadium at Gate A right now."

Jamison searched the building plans in her head and prayed she was remembering them correctly. "Stay against the outside wall and follow it to your right. When you pass Gate C you should be getting close to me so approach slowly. I'll let you know when you enter my line of sight. The gunman is under the stairs that will be on your right."

"We can see Gate B." Mel's breathing had increased as they sprinted toward her.

Jamison pulled out her phone and dialed Shea.

"Are you okay?" Shea immediately asked.

"Yes, and it's very quiet out here. I think maybe I hit him. Is there a flashlight in there?"

"Let me look."

Jamison could hear her opening cabinets as she told Jeremy what she was looking for.

"Got one."

"Great. Have Jeremy open the door and slide it to me."

The door behind Jamison slowly opened and a large yellow lantern flashlight slid across the floor.

"Okay. We can see Gate C coming up." Mel's voice came through Jamison's earpiece.

"I see you."

"I can see the stairs."

"Let's move in on him together." Jamison turned on the flashlight.

Her pistol held in front of her, she shined the flashlight into the shadows under the stairs and moved across the concourse. The gunman's body lay facedown on the concrete, his pistol inches from his fingertips. His body was large and beefy and he was dressed in jeans, a flannel shirt and heavy boots. She approached cautiously, kicked his pistol away, and touched his neck. She looked up at Mel and Nikki and shook her head.

"Well, crap," Mel said. "We won't get any information from him." She glanced around the concourse. "Where's Shea?"

Jamison started to talk but Mel cut her off. "Where's my sister?"

Nikki stepped in front of Mel, placing a quieting hand on her arm as she passed and addressed Jamison. "Hey James," she said sweetly. "You and Shea okay?"

Jamison gave her a weak smile. "Hey Nikki. Yes, we're both fine. Shea's over here." She led the way across the concourse to the blue door and knocked. "Jeremy, you can come out now."

The door opened slowly and Jeremy emerged, gun drawn.

Jamison put a hand up. "Everything's okay. The gunman is dead."

Shea came around Jeremy in a flash and hugged Jamison. Looking over her shoulder, she saw Mel and Nikki.

"What? Where?" Shea stepped away from Jamison and into Mel's arms.

Mel hugged her tight. "Are you okay, baby sister?"

"Shit, Mel. Baby? Really?" She pulled away and hugged Nikki. "I'm fine."

"Let's get out—" Jamison started as footsteps approached from both directions. Jamison grabbed Shea, pulling her behind her body as Heather, Sheldon, Carlton and officers from all three agencies arrived on the scene.

Jamison shook her head and pointed the flashlight at the gunman. "Heather, I think we need the coroner."

"On it."

"He was probably the only threat but let's get you guys out of here anyway," Carlton said, herding everyone toward the exit.

Carlton hugged Shea against his side. "I'm glad you're okay."

Shea hugged him back and then stepped away, giving him an evil glare. "You and I need to talk, Chief."

Jamison laughed. "You can beat him up later, cub. Right now, let's get out of here."

Shea slid her hand into Jamison's as they followed the group out of the tunnel.

"We're headed back to TPD to question Sullivan some more. We'll tell him his gunman is singing like a canary," Heather said with a smile.

Sheldon nodded. "Want to come with us?"

"You should come with us," Heather requested.

Heather would have paperwork concerning the shooting and Jamison would need to do everything she asked to help clear it up.

Shea squeezed her hand. "I can go with Mel and Nikki."

Jamison pulled Shea to a stop but motioned the others to continue. "Are you sure you're okay with that?"

Shea smiled. "I know you want to finish this so go do it. Then come back to me."

Jamison pulled her close. She wanted to kiss her and was surprised when Shea did it first. It wasn't a long lingering kiss but held a promise of what was to come.

"Will you be at Mel's?" Jamison asked.

"Probably."

"Make sure they clear your house before you guys traipse through there," Jamison cautioned.

"I'm sure they won't take as good care of me as you do but they'll try."

She gave her a sheepish grin. "I didn't mean to imply that."

Shea gave her another kiss and then joined her sister.

Jamison followed Heather and Sheldon back to their car. When Heather tossed an evidence bag over the seat, Jamison dropped her pistol into it without question.

CHAPTER TWENTY-THREE

Nikki turned in her seat to look at Shea. "That was an amazing game, Shea."

"It certainly was great to win."

"You looked awesome out there, little sister," Mel said.

"Thanks. When did you guys get here?"

Nikki laughed. "Just in time to see your bodyguard and her partners in crime climb the wall."

"Liam told me about that when I came off the field. Was she caught on camera? I'd like to see it too."

"I hope not," Mel stated. "She clearly forgot staying out of sight is one of our rules on a protection detail."

"Well, this wasn't a normal protection detail, was it, Shea?" Nikki asked, hinting that she saw something between Shea and Jamison.

When Shea didn't immediately answer Nikki continued. "Jamison is pretty sweet, right?"

"I enjoyed her company this week," Shea answered vaguely.

"That's not what Mom said," Mel stated.

"Where is Mom?" Shea asked, avoiding Nikki's eyes. She needed to get Nikki's attention off Jamison. They hadn't had a chance to talk about when or how they were going to tell Mel they were seeing each other but she knew Jamison would want to be the one to do it.

"She went back to the hotel after the game," Nikki explained. "Mel and I saw a Flagler agent and followed them to their debriefing."

"I stole Liam's earpiece and we were headed back in to help Jamison get you to her truck safely," Mel continued.

"I'm glad you guys found us."

"It seemed to me Jamison had everything under control," Nikki said, glancing at Mel.

"Did she kill that guy or did you guys?"

"Let's talk about the game. The Tigers defense really held them," Mel said, changing the subject.

Shea frowned. "See, that's something Jamison didn't do to me this week."

"What's that?" Nikki asked.

"She answered all my questions and didn't try to keep stuff from me."

"She broke all kinds of rules this week, huh," Mel said with annoyance.

Nikki sat sideways, watching both of them. Shea could tell Nikki knew Mel was irritating her with her criticism of Jamison. She wondered what else Nikki had noticed.

"Do you want to tell us about your week with Jamison?" Nikki prodded her gently.

Shea gave her a smile, glanced at Mel and then answered firmly. "No."

Nikki placed her hand on Mel's arm where it rested between the seats. "So you like her?"

"What?" Mel exploded.

Nikki's fingers tightened around Mel's arm. "How much do you like her?"

"Are we going to the hotel to see Mom?" Shea asked, ignoring Nikki's question.

"No. We're going back to our place," Mel responded. "Answer Nikki's question. Is there something going on between you and Jamison?"

"No," Shea answered.

"No, what?" Mel demanded.

Shea met her eyes in the rearview mirror. "No, I'm not going to have this conversation with you."

Silence filled the car and after a few minutes Nikki spoke. "I guess that answers the question."

Shea was glad the conversation about Jamison had stopped. She didn't care if Nikki knew something was up but she wanted Jamison present before she confirmed it to Mel. It really wasn't any of her sister's business who she went out with but Mel and Jamison had a different relationship and Jamison deserved the chance to deal with it however she chose.

Shea watched the streets turn to farmland as they traveled south out of the city. She was frustrated with her sister for not even asking where she wanted to go. She wanted her own clothes but now they were outside the city limits and she knew Mel wouldn't turn around. She felt like she was being held captive. She pulled out her phone and sent Jamison a text. *Headed to Mel's. Come get me when u finish. k?*

* * *

Jamison's phone vibrated with a text message and she smiled when she saw it was from Shea. She sent a quick yes back to her but then remembered she didn't know Mel's new address. She would text her when she finished tonight and see if she meant tonight or in the morning.

Sheldon's phone rang and she reached across Heather's arm and punched the Bluetooth button on the steering wheel. Todd's voice filled the car.

"Hey Sheldon. I've been digging up everything I can on Sullivan and you were right. Atlanta PD has him in a botched drug buy from about five years ago. He had no priors and claimed he was in the wrong place at the wrong time."

"Let me guess. They bought that story?" Heather asked.

"You got it, Heather."

"We have another tagalong tonight," Heather advised Todd.

"Who do you work for, Todd?" Jamison asked.

Todd laughed. "Mrs. Bowden is pimping me out. She says we're building interagency cooperation."

"That's nice. Is Sullivan connected to the Mountain Militia?" Jamison asked.

"Absolutely. He's worked his way up and is one of the officers now. His name is listed on their board of directors."

"Wait a minute," Heather interrupted. "The Mountain Militia has a board of directors?"

"Oh yeah." Todd's voice grew excited as he shared the data he had been compiling. "They're registered as a business with the state of Georgia."

Heather looked at Sheldon. "Did you know this?"

Sheldon shook her head. "I didn't but someone in the FBI might."

"So if all their business records are available to the public, we can look at anything? What type of business are they registered as?" Heather asked.

"Agriculture. And yes, their records are public but they're squeaky clean. As the FBI has already discovered."

"So we tell Sullivan his shooter is singing and we're tying this and his botched drug deal back to the Mountain Militia," Sheldon suggested.

"And see if he takes responsibility to clear the militia?" Heather asked.

"If he admits his part in all of it…" Todd paused but they could hear his fingers flying across the keyboard. "The shooter was a hired gun and not connected to the militia but maybe I can find a payment between him and Sullivan."

Heather pulled the car to a stop outside the three-story federal building that housed the FBI offices. All three women remained seated as they silently listened to Todd typing and talking.

"There we are. Matching withdrawal and deposit only one day apart. I sent a screen shot to your email, Heather."

"What type of agriculture are they producing and who are they selling it to?" Jamison asked.

"And see if you can find a phone call or email between Sullivan and the hired gun," Sheldon added.

"I'm on it."

"Call us when you get something, Todd."

"Let's take what we have to Sullivan and see where it leads us," Heather said, climbing out of the car.

Jamison watched through the one-way glass as Heather and Sheldon double-teamed Sullivan. He had not asked for a lawyer and Jamison was sure he didn't want to create another link between himself and the militia by calling in their attorney. At first he wasn't willing to talk at all and Wallace had been happy to allow Sheldon to take over. Jamison could see his composure starting to crumble as Sheldon fed him each piece of the connection.

Eventually he agreed to tell them what he had done but he wanted a public defender first. So Sheldon and Heather left him alone.

Jamison rubbed her face as the three women sat down at the table with fresh cups of coffee. "We're back to the first question. What does the Mountain Militia have to do with the Tallahassee Tigers?"

As if Todd could hear her question, Sheldon's phone rang and she glanced around the break room to be sure it was empty. She hit speaker. "We're all here, Todd."

"Great! Here's your connection to it all. The Mountain Militia supplies a farmers market outside of Atlanta which happens to be where the Atlanta Wildcats football team purchases their fruits and vegetables."

"What?" three women said together.

"Several years ago this particular farmers market was involved in a DEA sting operation."

"What were they selling? Pot?" Jamison asked.

"Among other things," Todd continued. "This market was popular for the sale of organic fruits and vegetables but the DEA had discovered synthetic steroids being sold as well."

Sheldon rolled her eyes. "So let me see if I got this right. The Atlanta Wildcats are purchasing from a market that sells anabolic steroids?"

"Not only the Atlanta Wildcats but their beloved coach, Skip Mason, who pushed the issue and brokered the exclusive contract with this market," Todd explained. "And the contract expires this year."

"Skip Mason is being recruited to coach in the NFL," Heather reminded them.

"Yes, he is and he'd probably broker another deal with his NFL team and the market, especially if he's picked up by a team on the east coast." Todd lowered his voice. "And rumor has it, Mason needs one more National Championship title to secure his NFL recruitment since he's so young."

"He would be the youngest NFL head coach ever," Heather added.

Jamison rubbed her face. "Are we saying Skip Mason could be behind this?"

Sheldon shook her head. "Not necessarily. Clayton Thomas and the Mountain Militia stand to lose a lot of money if Skip Mason is unable to broker another contract with their distributor."

"Todd, do we have anything substantial to prosecute any of this?" Jamison asked.

"Not today."

"Okay." Jamison looked at Heather and Sheldon. "Let's hang everything that happened today on Sullivan and see if he wants to pass the buck."

"Thanks, Todd, for the information. Can you get us the reports from the DEA sting operation? I'd like to know the outcome," Heather requested.

Sheldon then dialed Wallace who had disappeared after turning Sullivan over to them. After a several minute conversation she hung up. "Wallace got our two vendor boys to

ID Sullivan so we can tie him to the explosives. He's getting a Federal warrant to search Sullivan's residence—which happens to be the militia's compound."

Jamison sighed. "You'll only be searching for explosives though, right? This won't include steroids or anything connecting them to Skip Mason."

Sheldon nodded. "Right. All we're working with right now are the explosive devices left in the stadium and anything from earlier in the week. We should hear back soon if the explosives are all from the same batch."

Jamison looked at Heather. "Don't they test college athletes for anabolic steroids?"

"Yes, but if they're using organically grown items to boost the steroids that are naturally in your body it wouldn't show up on the testing."

"So technically they aren't doing anything illegal then?" Sheldon asked.

"I'm not an expert on this but my thought would be no, it's not illegal but they aren't going to get the same dramatic results either."

"But it still gives them an edge," Sheldon stated as she stood. "Let's go see if Sullivan's public defender has arrived yet."

* * *

Shea softly closed the door to the spare bedroom at Mel and Nikki's house and climbed into bed. When she'd finally gotten a moment alone to text Jamison, she could have cried at the dead battery on her phone. She couldn't even get the damn thing to power up. The stupidest part was that she didn't even have Jamison's number to call her from another phone. She knew Mel and probably even Nikki had Jamison's number but as badly as she wanted to talk with Jamison she couldn't bring herself to ask them. She knew she'd see Jamison in the morning.

Even so, she might ask Nikki to borrow her cell phone in the morning. She crossed her arms behind her head, knowing sleep would be slow without her connection to Jamison. She replayed the last twelve hours in her mind. The ins and outs of the ballgame and then her fear hiding in the closet while Jamison exchanged gunshots with the shooter. She still wondered if Jamison had killed him or not. Not that it mattered. She had known Jamison would do whatever was necessary to keep her safe. She missed the comfort of having her nearby.

* * *

"We're headed for Mexican food. Want to join us?" Heather asked Jamison as they climbed into the car.

Sullivan's attorney had arrived but Sullivan still refused to talk. Probably on his recommendation. Sheldon explained a couple things to him about how his prosecution was going to go and which charges she had him nailed on. He'd tried not to look concerned but Jamison, watching through the glass, had seen a few stutters in his facial expressions. Special Agent Wallace was pushing full force into the Mountain Militia and it looked like his search warrant was going to be approved. Sheldon asked him to call her when it was a go so she could accompany him and he had agreed.

Jamison checked her phone and was surprised to see Shea had not responded to her earlier text. It had been over an hour since she had sent it. She dialed Shea's number. If Shea was ready to be picked up, she was certainly willing. She didn't want to go back to her empty apartment. Immediately Shea's voice mail kicked in telling Jamison she was on the other line or her phone was turned off. She quelled her first instinct to panic knowing Shea was with Mel and Nikki. Maybe she'd turned off her phone to get some much-needed sleep. She could call Mel but Shea would be safe at Mel's so she should leave her alone for the night. She'd see her in the morning.

"So?" Sheldon glanced over the seat when Jamison pulled the phone from her ear.

"Yeah, sure. I'm starving."

"Your girl not answering?"

Jamison shrugged. "She's with her sister and her partner. Both are Flagler agents so I know she's safe. I'm not worried."

"No, you don't sound worried," Sheldon said sarcastically.

* * *

Jamison winced at the emptiness in her apartment. She was trying hard not to let Shea's silence occupy too much of her concentration. Dinner with Sheldon and Heather had been a recap of the entire case and they all agreed something was missing. McGomery was behind bars and would stay there for a while. Charges for stalking, breaking and entering and possession of explosives would ensure he didn't get time served when his case finally went to trial. Scooter and his vendor pal would spend some time in jail for their stupidity but none of the other arrests from the game had panned out to be involved in this case. Sullivan was looking at the most time at this point. He had finally admitted he solicited Scooter to plant the explosives but claimed he never planned to detonate them. What he had planned wasn't something he or his lawyer were willing to share. If there was a connection to Skip Mason it probably wouldn't be easy to find. Sheldon was already talking about forming a task force and it could take months to develop any leads.

She typed the last line on her incident report and sent it to Bowden. An agent-involved shooting was a big deal, but with Heather's report it shouldn't even require an investigation. Bowden had already informed her that she would be seeing a shrink before returning to duty. Nothing she didn't expect. She hadn't planned to kill the man but she had been willing to do whatever it took to keep Shea safe and she would again, if this wasn't over.

She dropped fully clothed onto the couch. Lifting her arms above her head she stretched from end to end. She closed her eyes and willed sleep to come. Sheldon had agreed to allow Jamison and Heather to accompany her when they searched the compound and she could call at any minute. Jamison wasn't sure Shea would be open to continued protection but she was going to suggest it. At least until the championship game was over in two weeks.

Her phone rang and she pulled it from her pocket. Sheldon.

"We decided to head toward Atlanta. It's pretty solid we're going to get the search warrant, they're just ironing out the details. Can you be ready in twenty?"

"I'll meet you downstairs."

Jamison tossed her phone on the table and headed for the bedroom. She took a quick shower, dressed in her black cargo pants, long-sleeved T-shirt and boots. Securing her backup pistol in the holster at her waist, she stepped out of her building foyer as Sheldon pulled to the curb. Jamison slid into the backseat of the black Dodge Charger and Sheldon roared away from the curb.

"I thought the FBI drove black sedans and SUVs with tinted windows?" Jamison asked as she lay down on the seat.

"Normally, yes," Sheldon answered, ignoring Jamison's taunting. "Tonight I thought we needed something with a little more speed."

"You might want to buckle your seat belt. Her foot has been stuck to the gas pedal since she climbed behind the wheel," Heather teased.

Sheldon took the ramp onto Interstate 10 with tires squealing.

"Honestly, Sheldon. Do you even know where the brake pedal is?" Heather asked.

"I do," Sheldon said with a laugh. "Want me to show you?"

"You'll roll Jamison onto the floor."

"And she won't be happy," Jamison added from the backseat.

Sheldon laughed and then she turned serious. "You guys are armed, right?"

"Of course. Is that a problem?" Jamison sat up, centering herself between the two front seats.

Heather nodded too.

"Not a problem. I just like to know who can back me up in a pinch."

Jamison lay back down. "Wake me when we get there." She closed her eyes and tuned out the conversation from the front seat. She liked Heather and Sheldon's banter. They seemed to have developed a friendship during their first trip to Atlanta, she thought as she drifted into sleep.

CHAPTER TWENTY-FOUR

"Hey Sleeping Beauty." Jamison felt a tap on her shoulder. She rolled toward the front of the car seat and looked up at Heather.

"We're about an hour away from the compound. The search warrant is about twenty minutes behind us so we're stopping for food. Want something?"

"Cheeseburger?" Jamison was surprised at the words that rolled off her tongue. She never ate cheeseburgers and especially not at fast-food locations but tonight that's what she craved. "With french fries and a Coke."

Sheldon slowed the car and pulled into the drive-thru lane. She ordered three combo meals and Heather passed around the food as Sheldon handed it to her. Pulling back onto the interstate, Sheldon maintained the speed limit.

"What happened to Mario Andretti?" Jamison asked as she bit into her cheeseburger. It was warm and juicy and flavorful, not at all what she was expecting.

Heather laughed. "I think she burned out about an hour ago."

"We're waiting for Wallace and the search warrant to catch up," Sheldon answered.

"Oh, right. Do we have a plan?" Jamison mumbled around her mouthful of fries. It felt like days instead of hours since she had eaten nachos at the Mexican restaurant.

"Sheldon convinced Wallace to go in soft and see where it gets us," Heather answered.

Sheldon swallowed her mouthful of food. "If they're trying so hard to be law abiding, then they aren't going to fire at the first car that pulls up. There's Wallace now."

The three women watched another black Charger fly past them and Sheldon slammed her foot on the accelerator to follow. Sheldon's phone rang and she pressed the button on her steering wheel to connect to the car's Bluetooth.

"You have Krews and Cannon with you, right?" Wallace asked.

"Yes."

"Good. You guys have FBI permission to make arrests or search anything included in the warrant."

Jamison raised her eyebrows at Heather and said softly, "Nice."

Wallace continued, "I could only get twelve agents not counting SWAT so everybody counts. SWAT will wait outside the compound unless we need them. If soft doesn't work we'll only have ten more bodies and from the size of this place we might be stretched thin. The numbers on Sullivan's address match a huge warehouse, not a house or cabin, so that's what we get to search. Unless we find something, then the judge will expand the search." They could hear paper rustling as Wallace pulled out the search warrant and read exactly what items they could search. "So, basically, any location you could hide explosives or anything related to explosives."

Sheldon nodded. "That's pretty wide."

"Yes, we're going to turn this warehouse upside down." He paused as his vehicle turned off onto a dirt road and pulled to the side. "Take lead, Sheldon. Show me how this soft touch works."

"You got it." Punching the accelerator, she disconnected the call. "Here we go."

Everyone was silent as Sheldon maneuvered slowly along the dark road. Jamison looked out the rear window and could see two black SUVs following Wallace's Charger. Jamison watched as they passed only trees on both sides of the road. Sheldon slowed to a stop in front of a large metal gate stretching the width of the road. The area was lit only from the quarter moon in the sky above them. Sheldon's headlights shone on a large white sign with red letters announcing they were entering private property. No trespassers allowed.

Jamison opened her door and quietly pulled her pistol from its holster, holding it beside her leg as Heather climbed out to open the gate. Jamison walked through the gate, scanning the area around them. Nothing but trees stretched as far as she could see. She was surprised there was no one from the militia watching the gate. Sheldon pulled their vehicle through and stopped as Wallace's car pulled alongside them with his window open.

"Let's keep a nice gap between vehicles." Jamison heard Wallace call between the open windows. "I'm feeling a little claustrophobic."

Sheldon nodded. "Probably a good idea."

"Call me before you check in with them at the next gate so I can listen to your conversation."

"Okay."

Jamison glanced around again at the forest surrounding them. She agreed with Wallace. The road was plenty wide for two vehicles to pass but with the trees so close on both sides it felt smaller in the darkness. She was relieved when Heather returned to the vehicle and they began moving again.

A mile down the road they came to another metal gate, this one patrolled by several men dressed in camouflage clothing and boots. The dusk to dawn lights lining both sides of the road gave the impression of daylight. As they approached, Sheldon dialed Wallace and left the Bluetooth open.

"Watch right and I'll watch left," Jamison said softly into Heather's ear as they pulled to a stop.

The young man who approached the vehicle did not carry a rifle or have a pistol strapped to his waist but both men on the other side of the gate did.

"Can I help you, ma'am?" he asked as he leaned toward the window, his young face barely showing signs of razor stubble. He moved his eyes quickly around the car, assessing each of the occupants.

"We have a search warrant for the warehouse."

He nodded as if expecting them. "Please wait a moment."

He returned to the gate and spoke to his fellow militiamen. Pulling a radio from his waist, he spoke into it and then returned to Sheldon's car.

"Please follow Adam." He motioned toward a black Jeep that had pulled into the road in front of them. "He'll take you to the split in the road and Mr. Thomas will meet you there."

Sheldon nodded. "Thank you."

The guard on the other side of the gate opened it to allow them access and Sheldon pulled slowly through. Jamison watched as each of their trail vehicles followed before the gate closed behind them.

Everyone was silent as they followed the Jeep deeper into the woods. As they neared the intersection, Jamison could see a large lit up area through the trees to her right, which she assumed was the warehouse, and a hint of the compound to her left. What she could see of the compound reminded her of Girl Scout camp. A large central building surrounded by floodlights and a speckling of smaller cabins. A campfire burned away from the buildings and Jamison could see the silhouettes of ten or so men standing around it.

Another Jeep approached from the compound and their previous guide turned and headed back to the gate. A hand emerged from the open passenger window of the new Jeep and motioned for them to follow. They turned right, moving away from the compound, and within seconds a large clearing emerged. The warehouse was covered with metal siding in a range of woodland colors that blended into the forest around them. Several floodlights pointed at the main entrance where two large rollup doors stood open.

Jamison could see a large open area with floor-to-ceiling stacked crates—and that wasn't even a fourth of the building. A solid door in the wall to the right led into the main warehouse. A tall, thin man, with perfectly styled gray hair, climbed from the passenger side of the Jeep and casually strolled toward Sheldon's vehicle. He was dressed in jeans and a flannel shirt and did not appear to have been awakened at this early hour.

"Good evening, ladies. I'm Clayton Thomas." His voice was smooth and he did not appear to be surprised or worried about their appearance.

He stuck out his hand to Sheldon as she climbed out of the vehicle and then to Heather and Jamison as they joined her. Once Sheldon identified herself as FBI, Jamison followed Heather's lead and went only with a first name.

"I understand you have a search warrant for my warehouse? Can I ask why?"

Jamison watched his face as Sheldon spoke.

"Robert Sullivan claims this address as his residence. He was arrested and has admitted to attempting to plant explosives at the Tallahassee Tigers game yesterday. We're searching for the location he used to assemble the explosive devices or any pieces used for the assembly. Were you aware of any of this, Mr. Thomas?" Sheldon rattled off the information like it had been rehearsed.

He looked convincingly surprised. "No. No. I've known Robbie for over ten years and I've never known him to mess with explosives or to do anything against the law. Are you sure about this?"

"Yes, we're sure." Sheldon glanced at Wallace approaching and inclined her head toward him. "Agent Wallace can go over the search warrant with you while we get started here. Please ask your employees to remain outside the building unless we call for them."

Clayton Thomas motioned for his employees to return to their vehicles while he turned his attention to Wallace.

Heather tossed Sheldon and Jamison a pair of gloves and the three women approached the huge building to begin their search. The other agents joined them and Sheldon separated them into two-person teams, assigning them to specific areas of the warehouse. Jamison followed Heather and Sheldon into the first of two offices. Careful not to touch or open anything that wasn't covered in the search warrant, she combed through every drawer in the desk and read all paperwork left in plain view.

She didn't send any more texts to Shea but checked her phone often to see if Shea had responded to her earlier messages. She refused to allow herself to ponder the what-ifs of Shea's silence. Though the search was much more civilized than anyone would have expected, she still needed to keep her mind on her task. If Shea was giving her the brush-off, she would have plenty of time to mourn her loss later. She was relieved to see Heather approaching with bottled water and gladly accepted one.

"Has anyone found anything?" Jamison asked.

"Nothing yet, but the bomb dogs are still about twenty minutes out."

Heather passed Sheldon a bottle of water as she approached them.

"Part of me didn't expect to find anything but the other part is very disappointed," Sheldon said, taking a large drink.

Jamison stared over Sheldon's shoulder, studying the layout of both offices. They were positioned against the outer wall to the right of the main floor. Both had glass windows covering the side so they could look out onto the warehouse floor.

Jamison took a step closer. "The wall is too thick."

"What?" Sheldon asked.

"Look through the window at the interior size of the offices. The wall in between the two offices is several feet thick." Jamison went back into the first office.

"Is there a bathroom in there, maybe?" Heather asked.

"If there is I didn't notice it." Sheldon walked toward the open office door and Heather followed.

Jamison tapped on the wall and it sounded solid. She stepped back and surveyed it again. There were no seams where a door might be so she felt around the edges of the bookshelf mounted to the wall. Nothing there either. She left the office and stared through both glass windows into each room. The wall was definitely too thick. It wasn't something you could tell at first glance because the glass window stopped a few feet before the wall, giving the impression the room was larger than it actually was. Heather and Sheldon watched her through the window.

She went back into the first office again. The mounted bookshelf had a thick braided rug covering the floor in front of it. When Jamison rolled back the rug she could see scuff marks on the floor in front of the bookshelf. Her excitement building, she began touching everything on the bookshelf, looking for a trigger. She pulled a bowling trophy toward her and stepped back in surprise as a hum filled the room. The base of the trophy was mounted to the shelf and when Jamison pulled it only the top had swung toward her. Like something out of a movie, Jamison watched one side of the bookshelf move toward her as it opened to reveal a small room. Flipping on the light inside, it only took her a moment to find the door switch for the other side. She pressed it and smiled into the surprised faces of Sheldon and Heather.

"Cool!" Heather exclaimed as she stepped out of the way of the moving shelf.

The three women stared at the contents of the room.

Sheldon took a breath. "What the hell?"

It was loaded floor to ceiling with explosives.

* * *

Jamison slid into Sheldon's car and collapsed onto the backseat. She was exhausted but they had managed to search every corner of the warehouse. Throughout the night the search had continued to broaden as they uncovered first explosives and then drugs. After they found the secret room, Jamison had begun referring to it as the wall of honor. Pictures of famous women in sports and politics with targets drawn over each face covered every inch.

"That was amazing," Heather exclaimed, climbing into the front seat.

"Your first drug bust?" Jamison asked.

"Not my first but certainly the biggest. Between the explosives and the drugs, we should get a Pulitzer."

"Personally, my favorite was the pictures of Shea," Jamison said sarcastically.

"I didn't realize she'd been on the cover of *Sports Illustrated* so many times. Impressive."

"Where's Sheldon, anyway? I thought she was right behind us."

"Wallace stopped her when we were leaving. I think he wants her to start the interrogations when we get back," Heather explained.

"I wish I could join you but I have a brunch date."

"Did we have fun, ladies?" Sheldon joked, jumping behind the wheel.

Agent Wallace rested his arms on the open window. "Thank you all for the assistance. That was a good catch, Agent Krews. I didn't think we'd be able to make Clayton Thomas squirm let alone arrest him."

"Is he under arrest?" Jamison asked.

"Well, he's being detained and I'm hoping for the best."

"Is any of this property in his name?" Heather asked.

Wallace shook his head. "It's not, but where he screwed up was claiming residence here. This has been his address of record for the last ten years. If the person listed as owner has not claimed this as his residence, then it won't be a leap to prove everything confiscated belongs to Thomas. His lawyer has already started pushing the blame off on Sullivan but with what we found today everyone that claims residence here will be facing jail time."

"I think Skip Mason just lost his supplier," Heather said, grinning.

"We'll definitely shut this place down but depending on the tests on the produce the farmers market might remain open," Wallace explained. He glanced at Jamison. "We'll follow the path as far as it takes us. At the very least I expect the Atlanta

Wildcats will have a round of drug testing before the game in two weeks."

"Thanks. Keep me in the loop if you uncover anything on the threats to Shea."

"The news media is all over this so I think Sullivan will be framed as the bigot he is and most likely take the fall for all of that." Wallace tapped the window frame. "I better get back in there. Sheldon, keep in touch with me."

Sheldon nodded, dropping the car in gear.

The women remained silent while Sheldon cleared them past the FBI agents who were controlling access at the entrance gate. The crowd of television cameras parted as Sheldon maneuvered the Charger through the middle of them.

Jamison was fairly sure no one could see them through the darkened windows of the Charger. "I guess the media is aware of something going on."

* * *

Shea rolled over and instantly grabbed her cell phone, forgetting that the battery had died the previous night. She groaned and tossed it back on the nightstand. Her body ached from yesterday's game but she knew movement would make her feel better. Pushing herself to get out of bed to find out what time it was, she stumbled to the living room still in her pajamas.

"Good morning, sweetheart," her mother crooned as she ran over to kiss her on the cheek.

"Morning, Mom," Shea grumbled. "Can I get a cup of whatever you guys are having?" She motioned to the cups on the table in front of Mel and Nikki.

"Sure." Nikki got up and went to the kitchen.

Shea followed her speaking softly, "Can I borrow your phone?"

"Sure." Nikki handed her a cup of coffee. "Accoutrements are on the table." She pulled her phone from her pocket.

Finding Nikki's address book empty, Shea handed it back to her.

"Something I can help you with?" Nikki asked.

"Do you have Jamison's number?"

"I do but she'll be here shortly."

"She will?" Shea looked around confused. "What time is it?"

"Almost nine thirty. She called Mel about an hour ago and got directions." Nikki leaned against the counter and watched Shea. "She did mention not being able to reach you."

"Yeah, my phone died last night and neither of your chargers worked."

Nikki grimaced, then nudged her shoulder. "You should've come and asked me."

She followed Nikki back to the dining room table and dropped into a chair beside her mother.

"That was a great game, sweetie."

"Thanks, Mom."

Shea positioned her head directly above her coffee and breathed in the aroma. She listened to Mel and Nikki analyze and argue about the football game while her mother joined in occasionally. Even after all these years, she knew her mother still barely knew the rules of the game.

"It works better if you drink it, little sister."

Shea looked up to find Mel watching her. "I'm just letting it permeate my body." Shea raised her head and sniffed. "Do I smell muffins?"

"You do." Nikki smiled at her. "Chocolate chip."

"Oh yum." Shea stood, picking up her coffee cup. "I'm going to shower."

* * *

Shea stopped at the entrance to the kitchen and watched Jamison leaning against the wall, cradling a coffee cup in her hands.

"Then I pulled this stupid bowling trophy and the entire bookshelf swung open. It was crazy," Jamison was saying with excitement.

Her face was flushed as she shared her adventure from the night before. She was dressed in all black clothing with black boots and the dark circles under her eyes gave away her lack of sleep. Shea couldn't pull her eyes away. She waited until Jamison had finished her story before stepping into the kitchen, and drawing attention to herself.

"I'm starving," Shea said, hiding her thrill of seeing Jamison.

"Next time try getting up before noon, little sister," Mel teased.

"Everything's ready." Nikki pushed Mel out of the way and carried a full plate of muffins to the table.

Shea followed the muffins and noticed the table for the first time. There was also a full plate of steaming pancakes, one of scrambled eggs and a bowl of fresh cut fruit. She glanced at Nikki. "Wow, this looks great. Is there anything left I can help with?"

Nikki smiled. "Nope. Take a seat and dig in."

She sat down across the table from Jamison and smiled. "Long night?"

"Yeah." Jamison returned her smile. "I tagged along with Sheldon and the FBI while they visited the militia compound."

Shea raised her eyebrows.

"I didn't get to tell you before the bullets started raining down on us yesterday but we took down one of the militia's board members during the game as well as locating more explosives."

"Wow," Shea said, glancing around the table.

She wanted to hear everything but she knew Mel would put a stop to it if she asked so she settled for filling her plate and watching Jamison.

The conversation around the table turned to light topics as they talked about yesterday's game and the upcoming championship game. Shea listened to the comments and participated when necessary but her mind was on Jamison and what their future might be. Jamison seemed a little shy and reserved but Shea blamed that on Mel and her mother.

When Jamison asked the location of the bathroom, Shea followed, waiting in the hallway. She pushed Jamison back inside and closed the door behind them.

"My phone died last night," she offered before Jamison could speak.

"Oh."

"Just oh?"

"That was a relieved oh. I tried to call and I'm glad you weren't avoiding me." Jamison smiled.

She smiled back. "We're okay, then?"

Jamison pulled her into her arms. "We're definitely okay." Jamison kissed her.

They both jumped apart when someone knocked on the door. "Are you both in there?" Shea's mother asked.

"Shit," Jamison choked out.

"Yes, Mom. Just a minute," she called before kissing Jamison again. She took Jamison's hand and pulled open the bathroom door. Sliding past her mother, she headed for the kitchen and her sister.

She stopped, making eye contact with Nikki. Mel was putting dishes in the dishwasher and looked up when Nikki touched her shoulder. Giving Shea an encouraging nod, Nikki put an arm around Mel.

Jamison immediately stepped in front of Shea. "Mel, I'm dating your sister. I really hope you're going to be okay with it since I don't plan on stopping anytime soon."

Nikki spoke first. "We're very happy for you both. Aren't we, Mel?"

"Yes," Mel croaked.

Shea dropped Jamison's hand and hugged Nikki. "Thank you so much," she whispered into her ear.

"You're welcome," Nikki whispered back. "She is happy for you."

"What's all the hugging about?" Shea's mother asked as she entered the kitchen.

"I've decided to pursue a professional football career after I graduate," Shea announced.

"What?" Mel exclaimed. "Where did this come from?"

"The owner of an NFL team visited the sidelines during yesterday's game and she made me an offer." Shea held up her hands to stop the flow of questions about to be hurled from Mel's mouth. "I told her I was a lesbian and if she was still interested then I was definitely willing to talk."

Shea tried to read Jamison's face and hoped she would be open to the idea. She wasn't willing to choose between her future in football and Jamison.

"What team?" Nikki asked, her steadying arm back around Mel's waist.

"There's only one team with a female owner," Mel cut in. "Since her husband died last fall, she hasn't relinquished the reins yet and some say she won't." She smiled at Shea. "That's really awesome, little sister."

"We're all so proud of you, sweetheart."

"Thanks, Mom." Shea said, giving her mother a quick smile before looking at Jamison.

"We have a lot to celebrate today." Nikki smiled at them all and began passing around drinks.

When everyone had a beverage in her hand, Mel raised her glass. "To Shea's future."

"To Shea's future," everyone echoed Mel's toast.

Jamison wrapped an arm around Shea's waist pulling her tight against her. Leaning her head close, she whispered. "To the cub's future."

Shea laughed and tapped her glass to Jamison's. "I look forward it. Can we go now?"

"Absolutely."

"I'll need to swing by the duplex and pick up some clothes before we go home."

"Home?" Jamison smiled. "That sounds nice."

Bella Books, Inc.

Women. Books. Even Better Together.

P.O. Box 10543
Tallahassee, FL 32302

Phone: 800-729-4992
www.bellabooks.com